THE FUN WAS OVER

Skye Fargo had enjoyed every night of the trip to Condor Pass.

There was Darcy, the lady painter who turned out to be an artist at love as she took all he could give and returned it with interest.

There was Henrietta, the voluptuous widow who stirred a hunger and offered a fulfillment as timeless and rich as the earth.

There was Athena, the ice maiden who played goddess but longed to become a woman.

But now they all were forgotten as Skye stared in the burning eyes of Molokah, the deadliest Comanche chief of all—while from behind came the click of traitors' guns being cocked and aimed dead at Skye Fargo's back. . . .

CONDOR PASS

by
Jon Sharpe

A SIGNET BOOK
NEW AMERICAN LIBRARY
TIMES MIRROR

PUBLISHER'S NOTE

This novel is a work of fiction. Names, characters, places, and incidents are either the product of the author's imagination or are used fictitiously, and any resemblance to actual persons, living or dead, events, or locales is entirely coincidental.

The first chapter of this book appeared in *Montana Maiden*, the eleventh volume in this series.

SIGNET TRADEMARK REG. U.S. PAT. OFF. AND FOREIGN COUNTRIES
REGISTERED TRADEMARK—MARCA REGISTRADA
HECHO EN CHICAGO, U.S.A.

SIGNET, SIGNET CLASSICS, MENTOR, PLUME, MERIDIAN AND NAL BOOKS are published by The New American Library, Inc., 1633 Broadway, New York, New York 10019

First Printing, October, 1982

1 2 3 4 5 6 7 8 9

PRINTED IN THE UNITED STATES OF AMERICA

The Trailsman

Beginnings . . . they bend the tree and they mark the man. Skye Fargo was born when he was eighteen. Terror was his midwife, vengeance his first cry. Killing spawned Skye Fargo, ruthless, cold-blooded murder. Out of the acrid smoke of gunpowder still hanging in the air, he rose, cried out a promise never forgotten.

The Trailsman, they began to call him, all across the West: searcher, scout, hunter, the man who could see where others only looked, his skills for hire but not his soul, the man who lived each day to the fullest, yet trailed each tomorrow. Skye Fargo, the Trailsman, the seeker who could take the wildness of a land and the wanting of a woman and make them his own.

1861—a land called Arizona,
south of Diablo Canyon.

1

"You just naturally say damnfool things, honey, or have you been working at it?" Fargo asked the young woman.

"Neither, thank you," she said stiffly.

He studied her for a moment. Bitterness robbed her face of some of its beauty, giving her an edge of hardness. But she was still uncommonly attractive, dark-brown hair curled in front, straight where it fell to her shoulders, a thin nose, nice lines to her face and well-formed lips. Tall, she had good, square shoulders and enough of breast to push the neckline of the maroon dress outward in a full, smooth rise. But it was her eyes that held him, seawater eyes, a blue green that shifted with her every change in emotion. They'd turned an ice-blue now.

"Do you remember what people said about it?" she asked.

Fargo nodded. It hadn't been more than a month back. "Hard words, mostly," he said.

"They said it was bound to end bad," she pressed.

"That, and more," he answered. "Some said fools deserve whatever happens to them. Others said that when you go into a grizzly's cave you're just naturally asking to be killed, and then some just called it a terrible thing and didn't want any talking or thinking about it."

"A good hiding place, that," the young woman said, and the bitterness drew her lips tight.

"But nobody called it murder," Fargo commented. "Until now."

Her seawater eyes shifted into blue green again, but they held steady, taking nothing back. "And that makes me a damn fool, is that it?" she said stiffly.

"Pretty much so, honey," he said.

"I believe I told you the name is Athena," she said, and he shrugged away the reprimand in her tone. "Well, I'm not a damn fool and I think you could hear me out," she speared.

He nodded. Her letter had promised him expenses just to meet with her outside Drovers Bend. "Guess that's only fair," he conceded.

"Please sit down. I have something to show you. It'll take me a moment to get it," she said. He watched her turn crisply, start into an adjoining room. The maroon dress hung nicely over a round rear, swayed rhythmically as she walked, a nice steady stride. Fargo eased his big, powerful frame into a small chair, a frown clinging to his forehead. He heard her snap open a suitcase and rummage through it, and the frown continued to stay with him, his lake-blue eyes narrowing in thought. Her letter, which had reached him at General Delivery in Elbow Creek, had been signed only Miss Athena. But her offer for his talents, plus expenses, just to meet with her had been more than inviting enough to bring him here. She'd wasted no time on small talk when he arrived.

"The Condor Pass massacre, you've heard about it, of course," she'd thrown at him.

He'd nodded. There weren't many who hadn't heard of it, an attack that made people shudder in horror in a land where horror was as common as chickweed along a roadside. Six wagons and an escort of outriders, twenty people in all, and there'd been only one known survivor. Even without his words, the grim evidence had turned the stomachs of strong men. Fargo remembered how, when he'd first heard about it, he'd thought it an unusually brutal attack, even for the Comanche. But in this dry and harsh place the Indians named Arizona, the unusual was usual.

The sun had been a little less burning that sabbath morning when the six wagons slowly rolled into Condor Pass, all big-wheeled Conestogas with reinforced springs and weighted undercarriages. They had halted in the very center of the high rock pass for sabbath services and everyone had gathered in a loose circle around the Reverend Eli Clairborne, an ordained Methodist minister, and his wife, Letitia, who led the hymn singing.

The Anderson family—George, Martha, and their ten-year-old son, Josh—along with Henry Corn and his two daughters, Amy and Beth, were seated in the front of the circle, the adults forming a ring behind them. Reverend Eli Clairborne was a hell-fire-and-brimstone preacher, delivering the words of the Good Book with impassioned tones and rolling cadences. The very rocks of Condor Pass rang out with the sounds of Biblical prophecy. He'd chosen a passage out of Genesis for this sabbath morning and in between the words "trespassers" and "forgiveness," the arrow struck him full in the mouth, traveling in a downward arc. It went all the way through his mouth, to halt deep in the back of his throat. The reverend fell with the arrow sticking out of his mouth as though he were sucking on a giant feathered candystick.

Someone screamed, only once. The confines of Condor Pass exploded in flying arrows and the sound of gunfire. The Comanche came from all sides, leaping down from the rock crevices, sliding over the tops of stones. A follow-up party charged in on horseback. Those trapped in the pass had little chance. Many never got to fire off a single shot in return and they were killed instantly.

They were the lucky ones. A good number were taken alive. They had hoped that surrender might keep them alive. It was an empty hope.

The escort outriders were taken first, as the Comanche rounded up their captives. The men were separated from the women, hands bound behind their backs with leather thongs so they could watch helplessly as the women were stripped, then raped, each one at least a half-dozen times. Only the two young girls, Amy and Beth Corn, were held aside and not touched. But they were forced to witness, and that would be seared inside them for the rest of their lives, visions no one could ever erase from their souls. After the Comanche had pleasured themselves enough with the women, they turned to another pleasure: torture. Some women were hung from an old dead tree by their hair until they passed out from the pain. Others had bear claws driven through their nipples, and Letitia Clairborne, the oldest woman in the group, was held with her legs spread-eagled while arrows were shot into her crotch until she resembled a deformed porcupine.

The men were dragged behind horses, whipped until their skins hung in shreds, and while still alive, their penises cut off. Little Josh Anderson was merely slammed into a rock until his small head split open.

Only one man survived, Charlie Sims, grayed and grizzled, the cook hired for the expedition. He had not been part of the circle of worshipers listening to the sabbath-morning sermon, a fact that later only fortified his lifelong distrust of religion. When the attack came, he dived into a narrow crevice, unseen and unnoticed. He was also the only man who, from the depths of the crevice, had chance to see the Comanche leader, who looked down from the top of a tall rock. But Charlie Sims crawled back into the crevice as far as he could go, turned his face to the stone walls. He stayed there after the Comanche had gone, his head so ringing with the screams of pain and terror that he thought the attack was still going on twenty-four hours after it had ended.

When he finally crawled from his hiding place, the sight that met his eyes made him too sick to run for another half a day. But he eventually gathered himself and retraced the paths he had come on in the wagons, hiding as much as running and the horror he had left behind haunted his every step. Finally, three days later, he met up with a team of prospectors who took him to a way-station town called Dry Patch. There he told his story to a traveling U.S. marshal. In time, a heavily armed burial party was sent out. They returned with shock in their eyes, to confirm that nothing old Charlie Sims had said had been an exaggeration.

Such was the massacre at Condor Pass.

Fargo clicked his thoughts off, but the same overwhelming reaction came to him again, as it had that first time he'd heard the terrible story. It seemed too vicious, even for the Comanche. Yet some would argue that there was nothing too vicious for the Comanche, and perhaps they were right. The U.S. government had bought Arizona from the Mexicans, but the red man had never recognized the rights of either seller or buyer. The Comanche, Navaho, Apache, Jicarilla, and Mescalero claimed this land and of them all, the Comanche demanded the highest price of those who trespassed. It was the Indian who had named this harsh, dry land where water came only in small doses, Arizona, "the place of little springs." Perhaps Condor Pass had been only one more warning by the Comanche, Fargo wondered, a message that the nature of hate was growing more fearful.

He glanced up as the young woman came back into the room, a piece of paper in her hand. "This is part of a letter written before the wagon train left Drovers Bend," she said. "Please read the last paragraph."

Fargo took the letter from her, noted that it was the second page of a longer missive. No scrawled, crude handwriting, he saw, but a fine, cursive penmanship, the script of an educated person. "Who wrote this?" he asked.

The young woman paused for a moment. "Is that important?" she said in annoyance.

His lake-blue eyes narrowed on her. "Don't play games with me, honey," he growled.

"Athena," she snapped, the seawater eyes turning a dark blue. "The letter was written by Professor Raymond Neils, one of the people on the expedition."

Fargo's brows lifted. "Professor?"

"He was an anthropologist specializing in Indian culture," she answered.

"Indian culture," Fargo grunted. "He saw some of it, didn't he?"

The young woman's lips thinned into a straight line. "The last paragraph," she said.

Fargo lowered his eyes to the few lines at the bottom of the page.

> While I fully expect to return, I am uneasy about some things in this expedition. There are no extra horses being taken along and I heard the cook, a Mr. Sims, complain that not enough essential provisions were being stocked for a trip as lengthy as this is destined to be. But then I may just be suffering the pangs of nervousness as well as excitement, for it is dangerous country into which we are moving.

The paragraph ended and Frago handed the letter back. The young woman peered at his strong-planed, intense, handsome face for some sign, found none, and finally threw the question at him. "Doesn't that seem strange to you?" she asked.

"A little unusual," Fargo admitted. "But maybe the

wagonmaster figured to pick up horses and supplies somewhere along the way."

"Nonsense. No wagon train counts on that and you know it," she snapped.

"Maybe so, but that still doesn't come out to what you're saying," he answered.

"It's part of it. No extra supplies or horses were taken because somebody knew they'd never make it beyond Condor Pass," she said. "And I've more that adds up to the same thing."

"You know how crazy that sounds?" Fargo asked.

"I know, but I'll stick to it. Condor Pass was planned to happen and that makes it murder, pure and simple," she said.

"Why? You have a reason?" Fargo pushed at her.

The seawater eyes shifted to a blue gray and he saw her smooth jaw tighten. "No, I don't have that yet, but I'll find it," she said tersely.

Fargo drew a sigh. "You didn't send for me to come all this way out here just to test out a lot of theories," Fargo commented.

"That's right," she agreed. "I want to hire you to help me prove what I'm saying."

"Prove?" Fargo almost winced. "How in hell do you figure to do that?"

"I'm going to do it all over again. I'm going to take another wagon train through Condor Pass," she said with a tone of triumph.

Fargo felt the frown digging into his brow as he stared at her. "I take back what I said about your being a damn fool. You're a plain, dyed-in-the-wool crazy," he said.

2

The seawater eyes slid into a deep green. A faint pink flush crept over her face and he watched the line of her breasts lift as her back grew stiff. "I am not a dyed-in-the-wool crazy," she said, wrapping each word in ice.

"Then you're doing a damn good imitation," Fargo said blandly.

"You go in for snap judgments, it seems," she bit out.

"You go in for wild talk, it seems," he returned.

"It's not wild talk," she almost shouted. "Condor Pass was planned to happen and twenty people were killed . . . *murdered.*"

"You keep using that word, as if saying it makes it so," Fargo remarked.

"It *is* so," she insisted. "Taking no extra horses and not enough supplies for a long trip is only part of it."

"What's the rest?" Fargo asked.

"The wagon train was organized by a man named Ellsworth Pond," she said, drawing a deep breath. "He lives here in Drovers Bend. But he not only organized the train, he insisted that he supply the wagons. Everyone that went drove a wagon he'd furnished. He bought their old wagons and gave them one of his."

Fargo eyed the young woman as she halted, waited for his comment. "Unusual," he admitted. "He say why he did that?"

"He said he wanted to be sure everyone had a wagon in top shape," Athena answered.

"That's reasonable enough," Fargo remarked.

"Ever hear of anyone doing it before?" she thrust back.

"No," he admitted.

"That's three highly unusual things so far, then," she went on. "There's more. Ellsworth Pond was supposed to lead the wagon train, but the night before they were to leave, he came down with a terrible fever. He was so sick he sent his cousin, Jake Pond, in his place. However, I've learned that Ellsworth Pond was up and about the very next afternoon, his terrible fever all gone."

"Meaning what?" Fargo asked.

"That he knew Condor Pass would happen," she snapped.

"And he just sent his cousin out to be murdered along with the others. Now, that makes no damn sense. Why would he do a thing like that?" Fargo said.

The young woman's lips tightened for an instant. "I haven't figured that out yet," she said. "I don't have answers for everything now. But I will," she added with vehemence, paused as she saw the skepticism in the big black-haired man's intense, handsome face. "I'm not finished," she said quickly.

"I'm still listening," Fargo allowed.

"The burial party that went back to Condor Pass found that every one of the wagons had been destroyed," she said.

"Hell, Indians most always burn wagons." Fargo frowned at her. "You're reaching, now."

"I didn't say they were burned. They weren't. They were just smashed, chopped apart," she said evenly.

Fargo let his lips purse as he watched her look slightly smug. "All right, that's not the usual thing," he admitted, growing aware that she was lining up a fair list of unusual things.

"Then we have Colonel Maynard Dennison," she said, and the bitterness in her voice grew harsher. "The colonel and his six troopers were all on leave from the Fifth Cavalry when Ellsworth Pond hired them. As he told everyone, Colonel Dennison was a very experienced officer in Indian warfare."

"You saying that was a lie?" Fargo asked.

"Oh, no. That was very true. Dennison led his Fifth Cavalry troop on Indian patrols for three years, especially against the Comanche," she answered.

"So what are you saying?"

"I'm not saying. I'm asking," Athena returned. "Don't you think a very experienced Indian soldier would have picked up one sign of trouble somewhere along the way? Did he scout Condor Pass, a perfect place for an attack, before leading the wagons in? If he had, wouldn't he have found the Comanche waiting?" She stopped flinging the questions to glare at him. "It seems plain that Colonel Dennison didn't do any of those things," she finished with a bitter flourish in her voice, the seawater eyes an angry green.

Fargo felt his lips purse as he watched her very attractive, angry, and determined face. She'd saved the most damning for last, of course, playing it for all it was worth. He wasn't sure how much it was worth, but it was strange enough, he had to admit. In fact, it was damned unusual, especially for an experienced man. He drew a sigh. "All right, you've lined up a list of pieces that don't fit right, but they don't add up to what you're saying, either," he told her.

"They add up enough for me," she snapped.

"You're saying this Colonel Dennison hired out to lead a wagon train into an attack and get everybody killed including himself. That doesn't make any damn sense," Fargo returned.

"Maybe his getting killed was an accident. Maybe

something went wrong, crossed signals or something," she countered.

She was good with answers. Fargo frowned. She'd a way of pulling out possibilities that couldn't be dismissed out of hand, and he gave her a narrowed glance. "Why would this Ellsworth Pond send all those people out to get killed in the first place?"

She gave an exasperated glare. "I don't know. I told you, I don't have answers yet. But he sent them out to their deaths and I'm going to find out why and I'm going to start by following the same route as the first wagon train," she said.

"What's that going to prove?" Fargo queried.

"First, that it couldn't have happened the way it did without somebody letting it happen. Then maybe I'll find out a lot more," she answered.

"Even if you have got hold of something—and I'm not saying you do—you'll still be going into Comanche country. That's enough to get yourself killed by itself."

"I'll take that chance," she said. "And the others all know the risks."

Fargo's brows lifted. "The others? You've got your wagon train lined up already?"

She nodded. "I posted bulletins in a dozen towns and got more than enough wanting to go."

"The world's full of damn fools," Fargo grunted.

"Six wagons," she said.

"Same as the first train," Fargo remarked.

"That's right," she said, a note of defiance in her voice. "I picked them as close to the makeup of the first train as I could. Even got another minister, a Methodist circuit preacher." She paused, her mouth tightening. "Except for the children. No children this time. I couldn't do that."

Fargo frowned at the young woman whose seawater eyes met his gaze. She seemed normal enough, still damned attractive, yet she was obsessed, driven by an inner burning. "Why?" he tossed at her. "Where do you fit into all this? What's your stake?"

She hesitated. "Justice. I want the truth known about this terrible massacre," she said.

He half-smiled, his eyes narrowing. She was handing him outside reasons when her every word was laced with the anger and bitterness of inside reasons. "Try again, honey," he said.

She frowned back. "I don't understand what you mean," she said.

"I don't buy your reasons," Fargo growled.

"They're perfectly good ones," she insisted.

"Then you can find another perfectly good man to scout for you," Fargo said.

"Not like you," she said at once. "You're the very best, I'm told, and I want the very best. That's all-important. I want to prove that an experienced scout would have picked up signs."

"That only shows how little you know about the Comanche," Fargo said. "Find somebody else."

"Why?" she exploded. "I've made you a damn good offer."

He nodded amiably. "The money's real good. The idea's real rotten."

Her seawater eyes slid into dark green. "Just because I want to prove something?"

"Because you're like a damn missionary, all fired up with your own ideas, and I'm suspicious of people too wrapped up in their own ideas," Fargo said. "Especially when they're all talk."

"I'm sure I can prove it," she said.

"And you'll put anybody's neck on the line just for your own suspicions," he said.

"It'll be no different than any wagon train. Everybody has their own reasons for going. I have mine," she said.

He uttered a short, wry laugh. "You're good at arguing," he conceded. "But it's still a wild-goose chase."

"No," she snapped. "All those highly unusual things mean something was very wrong."

"None are hard proof," he said.

"I didn't say they were. But when you see enough smoke, you know there's a fire," she countered.

Fargo turned thoughts in his mind for a moment. "Still don't like it," he said. "It's almost asking for a second massacre to happen."

Her eyes took on a hint of sullenness. "I've no more money to offer but I've something else," she said, and his eyes waited. "Me," she finished through lips that hardly moved.

Fargo let his brow lift. "You?" he echoed.

"That's right. You take me through, help me prove what I know is the truth, and you can take me to bed," she said, and glowered at him. He said nothing, his eyes studying her. "Dammit, Fargo, I've never made that offer to anyone before," she said, anger flaring in her eyes.

"Maybe you never had the chance," Fargo said blandly.

"That's rotten," she spit back, and the seawater eyes became dark green again. "I've had the chance, plenty of times."

He allowed her a half-smile. "I guess that's probably so," he conceded.

"Pardon me if I don't curtsy," she said, sniffing.

Mild amusement slid into the big man's voice. "Now, what makes you think that offer is going to make the difference?" he asked.

Her eyes grew smaller. "I've heard. The Trailsman has left his own trail."

"Maybe you heard wrong," he remarked.

She shook her head and a female wisdom crept into her eyes. "No, I heard right, and even if I hadn't heard, I'd know." Fargo let an eyebrow lift. "People talk without talking. There are all kinds of ways of saying things. It's in you, the feel of you, the look of you, the way you take in a woman." He smiled as she paused, waited, and he watched the exasperation grow in her face as he continued to say nothing. "Well, dammit? Is it a deal?" she burst out.

"No," he said quietly.

"No?" she exploded. "Dammit, why not? You never had such a good offer."

"As I said, the money's real good. I don't think the other part's going to match it," he commented.

He saw the fury explode in her eyes as her hand came up swinging. "Bastard," she flung at him. He caught her hand before it smashed into his face, spun her half around, and sent her stumbling as he laughed. She whirled back, her face red. "Get out. I don't want you in my sight. Get out," she shouted.

He laughed again as he turned from her. "Good luck, honey," he said. His hand had closed around the doorknob when she called out, her voice quavering.

"Wait, I didn't mean that," she called.

He turned, took a long step toward her, and she saw the lake-blue eyes were suddenly blue ice. Fargo's hand shot out, caught the top of the maroon dress, and yanked her forward. "You want my help, honey? Try being honest," he barked. "Start with a real name and a real reason."

She swallowed and he let go of the top of her dress, felt the softness of her breasts against his knuckles for an instant. Her eyes clouded and she glowered at him. Her voice was a low murmur. "Athena Neils," she said.

"Neils." Fargo frowned. "The professor who wrote you that letter, you said his name was Raymond Neils."

"He was my father," she said only a little less softly.

Fargo continued to frown at her. "Why'd you hold back on that?" he asked.

Her chin lifted. "That's only important to me. I was afraid you'd think that was all it was and just write me off," she said.

"Isn't that what it is?" he questioned.

"Yes, that's what it is for me. That's why I'm here. But there's more. It's not just my father being murdered. It's the truth of it. It's all the others who were killed, and Ellsworth Pond, and somebody paying for what happened."

Fargo studied her. She had a way of clinging to a thread of honesty when you dug deep enough. He felt his lips tighten as he turned everything she'd thrown at him in his mind. "You could be all wrong," he said. She shook her head at him. "Then again maybe you just might have hold of something," he thought aloud.

Her eyes brightened instantly. "Then you'll go along?" she asked.

"I didn't say that," he answered, and saw disappointment snuff out the brightness at once. "I'll think some more on it," he said. "This Charlie Sims, is he still in town?" She nodded. "Where I'll find him?" he asked.

"The saloon, where he's been ever since Condor Pass. He hasn't been sober in a month," she said.

"It takes money to stay drunk a month," Fargo said.

She shrugged. "Maybe folks feel sorry for him and buy him booze." Her eyes peered at the big man. "Why do you want to see Charlie Sims?" she questioned.

"I'm just naturally curious," Fargo answered. Displeasure at his answer was in the sullenness that came into her eyes. He tossed her a quick smile. "I'll be in touch," he said as he started from the house.

"When?" she called out.

"When I'm finished thinking," he said as he stepped into the late-afternoon sun and swung onto the Ovaro, the horse's starkly contrasting black-and-white markings gleaming in the slanted rays. He felt her watching as he rode casually away. She was a strangely intriguing young woman, he reflected, and more enticing than he'd let on. Maybe it was only the terrible anger inside her that was making her twist everything to fit her inner torment.

And maybe not. Some of the unusual things she'd put together weren't easily explained away. But there were more questions he wanted answered first. Then he'd decide about the rest. Except for one thing he had already decided. If he scouted for Athena Neils, he'd be collecting on part of her offer in his own way and his own time and it'd be a lot sooner than she figured. *If,* he grunted grimly and spurred the pinto on as the small town of Drovers Bend came into view.

He slowed again when he reached the town, rode along the wide, single street, taking in the sheep and cattle pens that fanned out behind the buildings, most of them empty. He halted before a wood-frame building that seemed more thrown together than constructed. The sign over the doorway carried a single word: SALOON. They didn't go in for fancy names in Drovers Bend.

Fargo swung from the horse and pushed his way in through the single slatted door of the saloon. His eyes traveled across the handful of men at a chipped and gouged oak bar, moved on to the half-circle of tables that extended outward. He found Charlie Sims quickly enough, the man sitting at a table near the corner of the bar. A gray, unkempt beard hid the lower part of a lined face with unruly gray-black hair. Charlie Sims had one hand curled around an empty whiskey bottle, the other trying to prop up a head that clearly preferred to fall down on the table to sleep.

Fargo walked toward the man, halted at the table. "Charlie Sims, right?" he said.

The man's eyes fought their way open to peer up at him. They were probably gray but they were so bloodshot they seemed red, Fargo saw.

"Want to talk to you, Charlie," he said pleasantly.

The older man's eyes struggled to peer at him and his tongue slid out to touch dry, cracked lips. "Talk?" he echoed in a voice dry as the dust of an Arizona desert.

"About Condor Pass," Fargo said.

Charlie Sims blinked, took a moment to let the words sink through his foggy senses. "No, not Condor Pass," he said finally. "No."

"Just a few questions, Charlie," Fargo said.

The man's eyes stared back foggily. "No, no talk. Wanna drink," he said. His head started to drop lower.

"I'll buy you a new bottle after we talk, Charlie," Fargo said.

Charlie Sims' head lifted and he peered at the big man, tried to see through his bloodshot eyes. "New bottle?" he repeated.

"That's right, after we talk. But first you have to sober up so we can talk and you can remember right," Fargo said pleasantly.

Charlie Sims frowned with the strain of trying to think. "Don't know. Don't want to be sober," he muttered. The bleary eyes blinked again and his face twisted as he tried to focus more sharply on the big man in front of him. "New bottle?" he repeated.

"After we talk," Fargo said. "You've my word." He reached a hand out to the man. "Let's go outside, Charlie," he suggested.

The voice cut into his thoughts. "He's not goin' anywhere," it said. "Leave him be."

Fargo looked up, to see the man at the corner of the bar nearby, narrow eyes in a heavy face, a black beard, and a stocky, barrel-chested body. A second man stood beside him, taller, with an angular, jutting jaw and a dirt-stained kerchief around his neck.

"I don't see this is any of your business, friend," Fargo said mildly.

"I'm making it my business. Charlie don't want to talk about Condor Pass. You heard him," the man answered.

"Maybe he'll feel differently when he sobers up some," Fargo observed mildly. "I think he can decide then."

"I'm deciding now," the man growled.

"I want a new bottle," Charlie Sims cut in, his voice thick and his words slurred.

The barrel-chested man gestured to the bartender. "Give Charlie a new bottle," he ordered.

The bartender raised his arm to take a bottle from the shelf behind the bar when Fargo's voice cut in. "I wouldn't do that, mister," it said. The voice had been soft, just a notch above a whisper, but the bartender had been in his job too long not to recognize the deadly danger in it. He drew his arm down respectfully and Fargo's glance returned to the barrel-chested man. "You've good reasons, I hope," he said.

"For what?" the man barked.

"For not wanting Charlie to talk to me," Fargo said.

The man's eyes grew smaller. "I told you, I just don't want him bothered," he said.

"Just a little old mother hen, are you?" Fargo said.

"I'll mother-hen you, mister," he man said, and moved forward, his right fist coming around in a short arc.

Fargo blocked the blow with ease, drove a short, straight right into the man's midsection. The barrel-chested figure staggered backward with an audible expulsion of air. Fargo swung a looping left, the powerful deltoid muscles of his shoulder driving it forward. It crashed into the man's jaw, sending the stocky body spinning around, to fall against the bar. Out of the corner of his eye, Fargo saw others moving for cover, Charlie Sims falling from his chair, and then the second man was diving at him, stained kerchief blowing backward as he rushed forward.

Fargo half-crouched, brought up a short right uppercut, and the man's feet lifted from the floor as his head snapped back. He arched backward and crashed into a table, sending it skidding across the floor as he fell with it. Fargo saw the stocky one had recovered, dived at him, head low, a bull-like rush. Fargo saw a stream of red coming from the man's mouth as he danced to one side and the barrel-chested form hurtled past him, halted, started to spin around. Fargo drove a short, chopping, overhand right downward. It struck the man's cheekbone, splitting the skin instantly, traveled down to drive his upper teeth into his lower lips, and a gusher of red erupted from the man's mouth.

With a bellow of pain and rage, the stocky figure tried to strike back, swung both arms wildly. Fargo stepped backward on his toes and the blows fanned air. He brought up a curving right, balancing on the balls of his feet, and smashed it into the man's jaw. The barrel-chested shape quivered for a second, then collapsed in a heap.

Fargo whirled just as the other man, clambering back on his feet, went for the gun at his hip. Fargo's big Colt was in his hand at once, the motion almost too quick for the eye to follow, and the gun barked once. "Aggh, Jesus," the man half-screamed, clutched at his hand, which had become a red claw. He fell to one knee and Fargo was at him with one long-legged step, yanked the gun from its holster. His foot lifted, landed in the small of the man's back, and the figure sprawled forward onto the floor, another oath of pain escaping the man's lips.

"You've got five seconds to reach the door," Fargo said in a voice of quiet deadliness.

The man pushed himself to his knees with one hand, half-fell, half-stumbled forward, propelled himself through the single swinging gate, and disappeared.

Fargo turned to the others who lined the walls of the saloon, watching with respectful distance. The barrel-chested one was still unconscious, he saw. "Anybody else got any objections to my talking to Charlie Sims?" Fargo asked mildly.

"No, sir," someone answered, and Fargo holstered the

Colt, smiled affably. He reached down and pulled Charlie Sims to his feet.

"Wanna drink," Charlie muttered.

"After we talk," Fargo said, steered the older man out of the saloon to where the pinto waited. Ignoring the man's protests, Fargo lifted him up and draped him over the horse's saddle, swung up behind him. He rode out of Drovers Bend and Charlie Sims bounced, stomach down, on the saddle.

"Oh, Jesus, stop," the man gasped out thickly, but Fargo kept the pinto at a steady canter as he headed for a shallow river he'd noted just east of the town. Charlie Sims continued to gasp out protests and Fargo heard his cries growing more pained, his voice gargling in his throat as the horse bounded him on his bloated, whiskey-filled gut. Fargo reached the river just as Charlie Sims let out an anguished gasp; he reined in the pinto and pulled the man from the saddle. Charlie Sims hit the ground just as he began to retch, lay on his stomach, and heaved out great, retching gasps, staining the riverbank with the smell of rot-gut whiskey.

Finally, when he halted, his chest moving up and down with drafts of gulped-in air, Fargo swung from the saddle, picked the man up by the back of his shirt and trousers, and tossed him into the shallow water. Charlie Sims let out a cry of surprise and protest, but Fargo followed, grabbed him by the hair, thrust his head under the water, pulled it out, watched the man blink as he drew in breath. Six times Fargo plunged the man's head into the cold water and each time he drew it out, Charlie Sims sputtered a little harder.

"All right, Jesus, all right," Charlie Sims finally managed to get out as he spit water.

Fargo let him go, stepped back, waited as the man crawled from the river on his hands and knees. He watched Charlie Sims sink to the ground, finally lift himself up and peer at him. The bloodshot eyes were still bloodshot, but the fog was gone from them now, Fargo saw in satisfaction. "Jesus, mister, who the hell are you?" the old man muttered.

"Just somebody who wants a few questions answered," Fargo said. "About Condor Pass."

He saw Charlie Sims' eyes darken and his tongue licked his lips. "I told everything," the man said. He peered up at Fargo and his bloodshot eyes were suddenly full of horror. "Christ, I can't go over it again," he said. "I wanna sleep nights."

"Just a few things," Fargo said. 'I want you to remember, think back, before the attack."

Charlie Sims frowned up at the big man. "Before the attack?" he repeated.

"That's right," Fargo said. "Did you hear Colonel Dennison say anything about seeing signs of the Comanche?"

Charlie Sims stared into space for a moment, shook his grizzled gray head. "Nope. Never said it where I could hear," he answered.

"Did he scout Condor Pass before you started through it?" Fargo questioned.

"Nope. He just took us into it," the old man said.

"When Reverend Clairborne stopped in the pass for sabbath services, did the colonel say anything?" Fargo prodded.

"Hell, it was the colonel's idea to stop there," Charlie Sims answered. "He said it was a nice place to hold services."

Fargo felt the surprise cross his face as he peered at the old man. His eyes narrowed in thought for a moment and then he reached a hand out, helped pull Charlie Sims to his feet. "The Comanche chief, I hear you're the only one who caught a look at him," he said.

Charlie Sims nodded and his mouth drew back in distaste. "Tall, he was, sharp-faced, a scar running down the side of his neck, eyes like burnin' coals," he said.

"Christ, he just stood there lookin' down. I'll never forget that face." Charlie Sims shot a glance at Fargo. "You promised me a new bottle, mister," he said. "I need it."

"That's right," Fargo said. "Your two friends keep you sleeping out of a bottle?"

"Enough times," the man muttered.

"Who are they?" Fargo asked.

"Sam and Jimmy. They're good to me."

"Sam and Jimmy?"

"I just know their first names. They work for Ellsworth Pond," Charlie Sims said.

Once again, surprise touched Fargo's face and he tucked the information into a corner of his mind, gestured to the pinto. "Get on. I'll take you back to town," he said, and watched Charlie Sims pull himself onto the horse. Fargo rode the old man back to Drovers Bend as dark settled down, let the man slide to the ground in front of the saloon. He tossed him enough for a bottle of whiskey and Charlie Sims peered up at him with a quizzical frown.

"Why the questions about Condor Pass, mister? It's all done with. There's no bringing anybody back," he said.

"Bringing back's one thing. Setting right's another," Fargo said as he turned the pinto and Charlie Sims pushed his way into the saloon, hurrying toward his bottle and forgetting.

3

Fargo sat crouched in the blackness of the little room, his big form taking up the entire corner. On the narrow, hard-springed bed, the cover and sheet were rolled and bunched, as though someone were asleep there. He'd left the Ovaro tethered outside in the warm night, right under the weathered sign that read DROVERS BEND HOTEL. They'd easily spot the horse, he reckoned. They'd be searching for it, he knew. He'd seen their kind too often, different places, different faces, but they were all the same. They couldn't take what happened like men. They'd have to come looking for their revenge, the coward's way, out of the dark, sneaking, underhanded, ambushing.

The big man was a motionless form in the corner of the room, the Colt in his hand, as he waited with the silent patience of a nighthawk. He hadn't moved when his ears picked up the sound, the scraping of boots in the hallway outside the closed door, a clumsy attempt at stealth. He raised the Colt and his muscles grew taut as the doorknob was turned with a faint click. Fargo's eyes narrowed as the sliver of dim light crept into the room, followed by the stocky, barrel-chested figure. The man carried a carbine, he saw, and a second figure edged the first, his right hand bandaged. Fargo watched the first man raise the carbine, aim at the roll of covers on the bed. The shot exploded in the little room with a deafening roar as covers and sheets were sent scattering across the bed. Fargo didn't need to see the astonishment on the man's heavy face to know it was there.

"Goddamn," he heard the figure bark, saw the man whirl, bring the carbine around to fire. The Colt barked twice and the stocky figure caved in, slammed backward into the wall. The carbine fell from the man's hands as his caved-in form pitched forward to hit the floor facedown. Fargo shifted the Colt a fraction to the right, held fire as the other man stumbled, fled down the hallway, crashing into the wall in his haste. Fargo rose, stepped to the door, and heard him leaping down the flight of steps, listened until the fleeing figure was out of earshot.

He holstered the Colt, stepped back into the little room, and turned the lamp up. The stocky figure lay with his hands clutching his lower chest, now little more than a red-smeared, torn shirt. Fargo leaned against the door frame and waited. The sheriff arrived a few minutes later with a half-dozen curious onlookers to find the big man still leaning against the door. Fargo watched the sheriff bend down to peer at the lifeless, caved-in form on the floor.

"Jimmy Simmons," the sheriff said, straightening up to peer at the big, black-haired man. "You the feller he had trouble with at the saloon?" he asked.

Fargo nodded, gestured to the torn, bullet-riddled covers on the bed. "He tried to bushwhack me," he remarked calmly.

The sheriff followed his gesture, nodded after a moment. "I'll have to tell Mr. Pond. Simmons worked for him," he said.

"Reckon you better do that," Fargo said pleasantly. "Now if you'll just get him out of here, I'll go to bed."

Two men dragged the lifeless form from the room under the sheriff's directions and Fargo watched the small procession go down the hall. The sheriff paused, turned back to him. "What's your name, mister?" he asked.

"Fargo, Skye Fargo," the Trailsman said.

The sheriff's brows lifted a fraction. "Simmons should've asked," he grunted. "Maybe he'd still be alive now."

"Maybe," Fargo agreed as he stepped back into the room and closed the door. He undressed this time, pulled the torn sheets over his long, beautifully muscled frame, and let sleep come to him. But it didn't come well and he woke with the first light of the dawn, grimaced, washed his mouth of its dryness. He'd spent a restless night, waking too often with questions that refused to go away. He went downstairs, found the kitchen deserted, and brewed himself a cup of coffee from a pot with yesterday's coffee grounds. He sipped at it in the worn lobby, made a face at the bitterness of it, but it quickened his coming awake as the night's thoughts returned to circle inside his head. The damn thing was full of holes and suppositions, yet it had kept growling in the pit of his stomach like a bad case of indigestion.

The old cook's answers had done nothing to knock down Athena Neils' case, and he frowned at how the two men had been so determined to keep him from questioning Charlie Sims. Ellsworth Pond's men, he grunted. Another coincidence? Too damn many, and too many strange things. Athena Neils was right on that. Was she right on the rest of her convictions? Massacre in Condor Pass? Or murder in Condor Pass? Or maybe both?

His lips drew back as the questions continued to hang in front of him. Damn Athena Neils, he swore silently. Had she hold of a terrible truth? Or had it all been just a horrible combination of carelessness, overconfidence, and Comanche rage? Overconfidence, he repeated, the word shimmering. No one experienced with the Comanche could become overconfident, and Colonel Maynard

Dennison had been an experienced man. Everybody agreed on that.

But little else, Fargo pondered as another question darted at him. Was Ellsworth Pond interested in keeping Charlie Sims drunk and silent because of pity for the old man and his own feeling of guilt over what had happened? After all, Fargo reflected, his own cousin had been massacred along with the others. Dammit, every question dragged another one along behind it. Too many questions, too many strange things that didn't fit right. Something was wrong. He frowned. Something, somewhere, somehow. Too much, he said silently. He couldn't just turn away from it. Not him, and a wry sound escaped his lips. Athena Neils and her seawater eyes didn't know that part of him, but she stood to benefit by it and he'd not be telling her any of it. Not now. He'd the feeling there'd be time to talk of reasons before this was over. If she were right, he repeated again. If she were right.

The bitterness swept over him with a surge. Justice belonged to the dead as much as the living. Maybe more so. He knew that better than most men, had lived by that creed for too long to turn away from it now. The search for justice had been seared into him on a day he'd never forget. He drained the last of the coffee, set the cup down hard on the table. Outside, the town was fully awake now and he stepped from the dimness of the hotel lobby into the bright sun, squinted for a moment, and walked to the pinto.

He'd just untethered the horse when he saw the man step down from a light pony wagon and start toward him. Fargo's lake-blue eyes took in the man's well-tailored jacket, his carefully stitched boots. He had a medium frame and over it a smooth-shaven face that was a little too much of everything, too much jowl, lips a little too thick, nose a little large, forehead a little low. It gave him the appearance of a walking caricature, and as the man halted, Fargo saw his light-blue eyes move up and down his muscular frame.

"You Fargo?" the man asked. "The one they call the Trailsman?" Fargo nodded slowly. "The sheriff told me you rode an Ovaro," the man said. "I'm Ellsworth Pond." He paused, and when Fargo made no comment, he went on. "I just wanted to say I'm sorry for the way my men behaved."

"They paid for it," Fargo said.

"Yes, but it shouldn't have happened," Ellsworth Pond said. "My fault, perhaps. I let them be very protective of old Charlie Sims ever since the massacre. I guess they just got carried away with that."

"Guess so," Fargo agreed blandly.

Ellsworth Pond offered a small smile. "You're not a man to talk much, I see," he said.

"That depends," Fargo answered.

"Anyway, my apologies for what happened," Ellsworth Pond said.

"Not your fault," Fargo commented.

The man's smile took on just the right note of regret. "An exaggerated sense of responsibility, I guess. It's ingrained in me," he said.

"I'd guess you're real upset about the massacre at Condor Pass, then," Fargo remarked mildly.

The man's face set at once in a mask of instant pain. "It's haunted me ever since. All those poor souls, my own cousin among them. I keep wishing I could have done something to keep it from happening, but that's an impossible wish, of course," he said, and his hands fluttered helplessly. He stared into space for a moment, returned his glance to the big black-haired man in front of him, and offered another quietly sincere smile. "I assume something brought you to Drovers Bend," he said.

Fargo's lake-blue eyes speared him. "You asking or fishing?" he said blandly.

Ellsworth Pond held on to his smile. "Asking," he said.

Fargo turned words in his mind. He'd held back questions and decided to do the same with answers. "Passing through, 'less I find something worth my while," he said.

The man nodded. "Well, my apologies again," he said, and turned, walked quickly back to the pony wagon. Fargo watched him drive away and swung up on the pinto. Ellsworth Pond had seemed full of sincerity, perhaps a shade too much so, Fargo pondered. He'd been a little eager to explain how responsible he felt about his men and Condor Pass. People who felt deeply about something weren't usually so glib, Fargo mused. But then there were always exceptions. It was too soon to start making conclusions and he shook away thoughts as he swung the pinto around to the road that led him to the small house a half-mile beyond the edge of Drovers Bend.

Athena Neils opened the door and stepped outside as he rode up. Her lime-green shirt made her seawater eyes a light green and he took in the way it pressed out nicely in twin curves, smoothly rounded, modestly full, and pulling tight into a narrow waist. He saw her eyes instantly searching his face and he slowly swung from the saddle, watched impatience thin her lips. He let her wait as he smoothed a corner of the saddle blanket.

"Well?" he heard her fling out, and he turned to see her eyes glowering at him.

"There's enough," he said slowly.

Her smooth forehead caught a frown. "Enough what?"

"Enough that needs answering," he said.

He watched the light-green eyes light up. "Then you'll go along," she said.

Fargo nodded. "A man's got to stand by his principles," he said.

Athen's frown lifted. "Well, it seems I misjudged you," she said condescendingly.

Fargo smiled back. "Let's just say I'm taking your offer," he said. "All of it."

The frown descended instantly. "All of it? Why? You said it was a matter of principle with you," she flared.

"It is. The promise of pussy principle. I never turn my back on it," he said cheerfully.

"Bastard," she flung at him.

"No compliments, please," he said.

Her breasts pressed tighter against the lime-green shirt as she drew in a deep breath. They were still smoothly rounded against the fabric, he noted. "I suppose I shouldn't have expected anything more," she said with icy disdain.

"You made the offer, honey," Fargo said mildly.

"Dammit, you were going to walk away. I made it because I had to, not because I wanted to," she protested.

"You try to remember that." He grinned.

"I'll remember it, you can be sure," she shot back, and he tossed her another grin as he turned to the pinto.

"Be back in a day or so," he said.

"A day or so?" She frowned. "I expect the wagons to be arriving today."

"They can wait a spell, get themselves gathered up," Fargo said.

"Where are you going?" Athena asked.

"To get some help. This is still a damnfool idea that could prove nothing except how to get another wagon train massacred," he told her.

"It'll prove what I need to prove," she said, and conviction flooded her face at once; he wished he could share her certainty. But all he could share was the series of strange questions that surrounded the entire affair, and they'd have to do for now. Answers and certainty would have to wait. He started to swing up on the pinto when she called out. "What kind of help?" she asked.

"Help called Joe Pueblo," Fargo said.

"Joe Pueblo?" She frowned.

"An old friend," Fargo said.

"An Indian? A Pueblo Indian, I take it?" she said.

"You take it right. He knows the Comanche better than any man this side of the Mexican border. He knows how they think, how they plan, how they eat, sleep, drink, fight, and hide."

"How come?" Athena queried.

"He was captured by Comanches as a young boy and held for years until he managed to slip away," Fargo answered.

"Where is he?" Athena asked.

"A town called No Place. It fits its name," Fargo said. "You just relax till I get back." He paused, tossed a narrowed, thoughtful glance at her. "I met Ellsworth Pond," he said.

"Oh?" she returned. "I suppose he told you how responsible he felt about the massacre."

"Something like that," Fargo agreed.

"He's big at telling folks that. Most believe him. I didn't think you'd be taken in that easy," she said.

"Didn't believe him and didn't disbelieve him," Fargo said. "If it's an act, he puts it on well."

"He put on a good act when he was selling rotten beef to the army," Athena snapped. Fargo's brows lifted. "That's right. I did some checking on Ellsworth Pond. The army canceled his contract to sell them beef, but they never got a full conviction because the government's chief witness was found shot dead on a roadway."

"Interesting," Fargo murmured.

"Just interesting?" Athena speared.

"Swindling isn't the same as sending people out to be massacred, including his own cousin," Fargo said. "I keep asking why, what would he get out of it? Murder needs a motive, a reward."

"It's there and I'll find it," she said darkly. "I don't back down."

"I'm counting on that." Fargo grinned and watched her eyes flash instantly. He turned the pinto and slowly rode away, glanced back once to see her eyes still simmering as she watched him go. He smiled to himself. Athena Neils was becoming a most interesting package, too determined and too caught up in her own mission, but still interesting. She wasn't the kind to go back on her word, he was certain of that. She'd keep her bargain when it was over, but she'd delay paying up to the very end and he didn't intend to wait that long. As he rode over the dry, hard ground, he amused himself by wondering if she were as determined in bed as she was out of it. Or if she'd ever taken the time to find out for herself.

His random speculation helped make time pass, but his eyes never stopped moving back and forth across the land. He espied a line of Indians, mostly squaws pulling travois, and he caught the Navaho markings on the hides they carried. He still gave them a wide berth. There'd be a party of braves somewhere not too far away.

A terraced limestone formation offered shade for himself and the pinto; he rested, slept till the sun lowered some, and then rode on, let the horse move along a muddy stream. It had grown dark before he reached the collection of scruffy buildings that rose out of the flat endless land and he rode into the town called No Place. Even wrapped in the kind dark of night, it was a scroungy place and a glow of light proclaimed itself before he reached it. Guiding the pinto to the wood building, he was almost at the saloon when he heard the shouts from inside. He'd reached the hitching post when a figure crashed through the swinging door, propelled backward, landed hard on the ground, and lay still. Fargo dismounted as another figure followed, this one slamming into the hitching post, doubling over in a half-somersault, to hang there as if cracked in two.

Joe Pueblo was inside, Fargo reckoned as he swung from the pinto and entered the saloon in two long-legged strides. He focused on the knot of shouting, struggling figures in the center of overturned tables and broken chairs. At the bottom of the pile he espied Joe Pueblo's thick, black shoulder-length hair. Four men punched and kicked at him as they struggled to hold him down. A fifth one circled, aiming random kicks. "Owoo! Jesus, he bit me," Fargo heard one man yell, saw his shoulders lift as he pulled back. Fargo stepped forward, clapped a big hand on the man's shoulder, knocked him sideways, moved forward, seized another of the men, and lifted him to his feet. As the man frowned in surprise, Fargo's blow caught him full in the solar plexus.

"Aaaaagh," the guttural sound fell from the man's mouth as he doubled over, started to sink forward. He was on his way to the ground when Fargo's knee came up and smashed into the point of his chin. The man's head snapped backward as the rest of him fell forward. Fargo brushed the limp form aside, sank a blow into the ribs of another figure, and the man let out a gasp of pain, whirled, and suddenly disappeared. Fargo looked down to see Joe Pueblo's arms wrapped around the man's legs, pulling his feet out from under him.

"Son of a bitch," the fifth man shouted from outside the perimeter, swung a hard roundhouse right at the big, black-haired man's jaw. It missed and Fargo clamped a hand on the man's forearm, twisted, and heard the man scream in pain. Fargo's left came around in a chopping motion onto the back of the man's neck and the figure pitched forward. Joe Pueblo was on his feet now, lifting the last of his attackers up into the air. Fargo ducked as Joe Pueblo's powerful arms flung the man in an arc and he watched the figure crash onto one of the overturned chairs, smashing it into kindling wood.

"Jesus, what you doing here, Fargo?" he heard Joe Pueblo say as two more men rose from the tables, started toward them.

"Heard there was a fight," Fargo answered, his eyes on the two men, both with faces made cruel by rage. The nearest one cursed out of a thin slit of a mouth as he came in, and Fargo saw his hand go down to the holster at his hip. "Don't do it, mister," Fargo breathed.

The man paused, but only for an instant, enough to fling defiance with his eyes. He yanked the gun from the holster, had it almost raised when Fargo's big Colt seemed to fly into his hand and fire at the same moment. The man's mouth fell open and he shuddered, staggered two steps backward. The gun fell from his hand as his right arm went stiff and he stared down in disbelief at the line of red across the side of his ribs. He clutched a hand to it as he sank to the floor and gasped out cries for help. The other man had halted, stared at the barrel of the big Walker Colt that was aimed at his chest. He swallowed, shrank back, fear filling his face.

"Drop the gun, mister," Fargo heard the voice cut in, and his eyes flicked to the door of the saloon to see the man there, a carbine in his hands, a star-shaped silver badge pinned to the front of a hide vest. Fargo glanced at Joe Pueblo. The Indian's eyes, small and black in a wide, flat face, looked almost sheepish as he shrugged his powerful shoulders under the loose, dark-green buttonless shirt he wore.

"Sheriff man," he murmured.

Fargo's eyes went to the sheriff as the man gestured to the onlookers. "Get that man over to Doc Hodge while he's still breathing," he ordered. He brought his carbine up a fraction to level it at the Trailsman's chest. "I said, drop your gun," he repeated.

Fargo scanned the man's face and saw tired eyes, the

eyes of a man who wanted no more than to do his job with the least amount of trouble. Fargo eased the big Colt into its holster, the move a message of its own, part compromise, part warning, and he watched the sheriff's face. The man's lips pursed for a moment; Fargo saw him accept the compromise and he grunted in silent satisfaction. He'd read the sheriff correctly. The man was happy to sidestep real trouble and Fargo saw him swing his glance to Joe Pueblo.

"I warned you, dammit," the sheriff said. "I told you next time you caused trouble it'd be six months in jail."

"Never heard of one man picking on five," Fargo remarked calmly, bending the truth, particularly when Joe Pueblo was involved.

"Well, now you have. He comes into town once a month and starts a fight," the sheriff said. "Who're you, mister?"

"Fargo . . . Skye Fargo. I came looking for Joe Pueblo," the Trailsman answered.

"Well, you can talk to him in jail," the sheriff snapped.

"I'll take him off your hands," Fargo offered. "Put him in jail and you'll be feeding him for six months."

The sheriff's eyes narrowed as he turned the offer in his mind. "How do I know you'll keep him out of here for six months?" he growled.

"My word on it," Fargo said, let the sheriff take another minute to study him. "Even in jail he'll be a bushel of trouble and you know it," he pressed.

The man lowered the carbine. "Yeah, I know it," he muttered. "All right, he's yours. But he shows up in town and I'll come looking for you," the man said.

Fargo nodded solemnly, played out the little charade to let the man maintain his front. They both understood the threat was but a hollow gesture. Fargo nodded to Joe Pueblo. "Outside," he said, and the Indian moved ahead of him from the saloon, moccasined feet noiseless, his powerful, chunky body held straight. Outside, Joe Pueblo swung effortlessly onto a dark-brown gelding with a white blaze, waited as Fargo mounted the pinto and moved alongside him. The Indian's black eye caught a glint of moonlight and Fargo saw the twinkle in their depths.

"Glad you come along, Fargo," Joe Pueblo said.

"I'll damn well bet you are," Fargo said. "Haven't changed any, have you?"

Joe Pueblo's flat, dark-hued face somehow managed to look injured. "I go town once a month. Some bad-mouth always say something," he explained.

"Which is just what you want," Fargo commented. Joe Pueblo's mouth touched a moment's smile that disappeared as quickly as it had come. "You've some gear to take?" Fargo asked.

The Indian nodded and led the way to where a small tent poked up over a cluster of echeveria. "Talk, Fargo," he said as he began to take down the tent and gather his few belongings.

"Need your help, Joe," Fargo said.

"Must be something hard," Joe Pueblo said wryly.

"Good pay." Fargo chuckled. "Better than six months in jail."

"Maybe," Joe Pueblo commented with wary wisdom as he finished wrapping everything into a small, flat packet and swung onto the dark-brown gelding.

"It's Comanche," Fargo said, watched the Indian's black eyes shoot a quick glance at him, instant interest in their almost impenetrable depths.

"We ride. You talk," Joe Pueblo said, and Fargo nodded agreement as he led the way back along the road that would eventually return to Drovers Bend.

"The Condor Pass massacre, you know about it, Joe?" Fargo asked.

"I heard. Very bad. Comanche," the Indian said.

"Maybe more bad than we know," Fargo said. Joe

Pueblo tossed him a quick frown. "I'll give it to you from the beginning, just the way I came into it," Fargo said, and began with Athena and all she had told him to support her convictions. He recounted how he'd questioned Charlie Sims and finished with Athena's plan to take another wagon train through Condor Pass to prove her certainties. There was silence when he ended, except for the soft sound of the horse's hooves; as always, Joe Pueblo's flat, impassive face revealed nothing. Fargo rode along until his own impatience got the better of him.

"All right, dammit, what're you thinking?" he barked.

"I think maybe I take the six months in jail," Joe Pueblo said.

"Nobody likes a smart-ass Indian," Fargo muttered.

"Nobody needs a damnfool friend," Joe Pueblo returned.

Fargo let a loud sigh escape him. "Okay, so much for that. What else?" he said.

"This wagon-train girl, maybe she so full of hurting inside she can't see straight," Joe offered.

"I thought about that and it's partly true, I'm sure. But what about all the things that don't make sense?" Fargo asked. "Too many, no?"

Joe Pueblo nodded without changing expression. "All right, too many," he agreed.

"Now, you going to answer some questions?" Fargo prodded.

"Ask," Joe grunted, and seemed to sit the gelding as though he had grown there.

"Why didn't the Comanche burn the wagons as they usually do? They smashed these. Does that have any special Comanche meaning?" Fargo questioned.

Joe Pueblo took a moment to answer. "No," he said finally. "Very strange. Comanche not one to change ways."

"Yet they did this time," Fargo said. "What do you

know about a Comanche chief, very tall, a scar running down the side of his neck?"

Joe Pueblo's small, black eyes grew smaller and he spat out the word. "Molokah," he said. "Very bad man. Even Comanche call him the cruel one."

"Molokah," Fargo echoed, turning the name on his tongue as he remembered how old Charlie Sims had spoken of eyes that burned with hate.

"The old cook saw him?" Joe asked.

"Just a fast look, but enough to remember," Fargo said, and tossed out another question. "This territory is west of Comanche hunting ground," he said. "Why is he here?"

"Molokah wants Comanche to rule far. He wants to be chief of chiefs," Joe Pueblo said.

"Ambition and hate. Bad combination," Fargo muttered, and drew a grunt of agreement from Joe Pueblo. They rode till midnight, when Fargo felt the weariness pulling at him and halted behind a deep-grained rock. With Joe Pueblo rolled cocoonlike into an Indian blanket nearby, Fargo slept till dawn slowly stretched itself over the flatland. He rode at a steady pace through most of the morning, halted near noon to take a notepad from his saddlebag and tear a page out. "We'll need more outriders," he muttered as he printed words in large letters across the sheet of paper. Finished, he read the simple announcement again:

OUTRIDERS NEEDED FOR WAGON TRAIN
ANYBODY INTERESTED BE
HERE AT 4 O'CLOCK

He passed the note over to Joe Pueblo. "Take it into Drovers Bend when we get near there. Put it up outside the saloon," he said, and Joe folded the sheet of paper into his waistband. Fargo saw the small house come into view, almost hidden by the semicircle of the six big wagons. Four Conestogas, he noted, and two high-sided hay wagons outfitted with closed canvas tops that made them resemble a poor-man's Conestoga.

"I'll go on into town," Joe Pueblo said, veering off, but Fargo waved him back.

"In a minute," he said. "I want Athena Neils to meet you."

Joe swung back alongside him as they reached the first wagon and Fargo saw Athena emerge from the front of it. He halted, swung from the pinto, and she stepped to the ground and hurried toward him. He watched the way her breasts, under a loose, white blouse demurely buttoned, swayed rhythmically, still smoothly rounded with no hint of nipple. Her eyes went to the figure on the dark-brown gelding. "Joe Pueblo," Fargo introduced.

"Hello," Athena said brightly, and flashed a welcoming smile. It brought no response from the flat, impassive face and Fargo laughed inside himself. "Fargo told me about you," Athena said.

Joe Pueblo allowed a short nod.

She tried again, keeping the bright smile. "He said you'd be of real help."

"Maybe," Joe grunted.

Her seawater eyes, more blue than green now, stayed on Joe Pueblo as she maintained her smile. "I'm sure you will be," she offered.

"Maybe," he said, glanced at Fargo. "I'll go to town now," he said, wheeled the horse, and cantered away.

Athena dropped her smile as she faced Fargo. "Regular chatterbox, isn't he?" she said tartly.

"He talks when you come across real to him," Fargo said.

"What's that supposed to mean?" she frowned.

"You were trying too hard. You talked down to him," he told her, and saw protest leap into her eyes.

"I wasn't doing any such thing," she said.

"Maybe you didn't even know it yourself. I'll give you that much," he said. "But you were doing it." He saw the moment of dismay come into her eyes. "Men such as Joe Pueblo don't listen to words alone. They pick up what surrounds the words. Their instincts and senses still work. They haven't been overcivilized," Fargo told her.

She studied him for a moment. "Where does that leave you?" she slid at him.

"Wherever you want it to," he said.

She turned away for a moment. "Can we leave this afternoon?" she asked, her eyes scanning the other wagons.

"Not likely. Why the hurry?" he said.

"I want to get moving. Everyone's here and waiting," she snapped, but he caught the hint of nervousness in her voice.

"Any other reason?" Fargo said calmly.

Her quick glance was one of impatience. "I had another run-in with Ellsworth Pond. I'd just like us to get going," she said.

"Another run-in? You never told me you'd had any before?" Fargo frowned.

"One or two, nothing important," she said too glibly.

Fargo's eyes narrowed. "Are you telling me he knows what you're trying to prove?" he barked.

"Not exactly," she said.

"Not exactly? What the hell does that mean?" Fargo pressed.

"I told him his wagon train wasn't run right and that I'd prove a train could get through if it were run properly. That's all I said. That's what I've told everyone. I haven't said anything about what I really think."

"Maybe it just comes across anyway," Fargo said grimly.

Athena shrugged away the remark. "I'll introduce you to the others," she said, and started toward the nearest wagon. "I've told them I hired you because you were the very best."

"You tell them what you were paying?" Fargo asked blandly. He saw the faint pink glow touch her cheeks and her lips tighten as she ignored his question. Two men stepped from the Conestoga as they approached, both pushing middle age, both a little thick around the middle.

"Abe Sprain," Athena said, gesturing to one of the men, a pleasant-faced man with a balding hairline. "And Jeff Howard," she said of the other one, shorter in build with an earnest expression that just edged being dour. Fargo shook hands with both men.

"Glad you'll be taking us through," Abe Sprain said. "Miss Athena said you might have some questions."

"I have. What makes you risk your scalps?" Fargo asked bluntly.

Both men returned wry smiles. "You don't mince words, do you?" Abe Sprain said.

"Never saw the need for it," Fargo answered.

"There's silver out beyond Condor Pass, in Black Canyon, more than enough to let a man live the rest of his life in comfort. Jeff and me, we've hardscrabbled too long. It's a last chance at the jackpot for us," Abe Sprain said.

"We'll pull our weight. We can handle a wagon and shoot straight," Jeff Howard put in.

Fargo nodded, decided the man was being honest enough. "Good," he said, and followed Athena to the next wagon, one of the converted hay wagons. A well-built young man, strong-featured, with a black, somewhat shaggy beard, waited beside a slender woman.

"Herb and Mary Atkinson," Athena said, and Fargo's eyes lingered for a moment on the young woman. She was, he quickly saw, one of those women who made a career of plainness, brown hair pulled back severely making her face slightly pinched, her breasts flattened by a tight undergarment, her dress a dull gray. "Herb and Mary are headed for California," Athena said.

"The promised land." Herb Atkinson smiled.

Fargo's eyes went to the young woman. "Can you handle a rifle?" he asked.

"Yes," she said, but there was a moment's hesitation in her voice.

"But what?" Fargo prodded.

"Mary comes from a Quaker background," her husband cut in. "Firearms still bother her."

"She'd best get unbothered," Fargo said as he moved to the next wagon, a Conestoga. A man in a black vest and shirt sleeves came around from the other side of the wagon, turned on an expansive smile. "Welcome, my dear," he said to Athena in a booming, preacher's voice, turned his eyes on Fargo. "Greetings, brother. I'm Reverend Joseph Moreland," Fargo's glance went past the minister to the woman who had appeared behind him. "My good sister, Judith," the reverend introduced. Judith moved into the open, a woman in her early forties, Fargo guessed, but with a plump face that gave her a baby-faced appearance. A loose dress didn't hide a matching body of plump proportions.

"Judith and I are both excited about this opportunity to carry the Lord's word into new places," Reverend Moreland proclaimed. Judith smiled happily in agreement.

"Preaching's your job," Fargo said. "Where does Judith fit in?"

"Judith is my right hand. Not only those of the cloth carry the Word, Brother Fargo. We are all commanded to carry the good news. Judith does so in song and music. She plays the organ and leads the hymn singing," the reverend said pridefully.

Fargo's glance went to the back of the Conestoga where the square end of a large wooden piece jutted out. "That a pump organ you're carting?" he asked.

"Indeed it is," the reverend said.

Fargo's eyes traveled along the bottom of the wagon, scanning the hickory axle bar where it fitted into the skeins, paused at the place where the hubs rested on the axle gear. "You're overloaded," he said. "Leave the organ."

"Impossible," Reverend Moreland boomed. "It is Judith's call to praise the Lord in song. 'Sing forth the honor of His name,' Psalm Sixty-six, verse two."

"How else could I do my task?" Judith Moreland said just as Fargo was beginning to wonder if she ever spoke up. She had a clear, sweet voice that didn't really go with her plump face.

"Get a harmonica," Fargo said.

"I'm sure one pump organ isn't going to make all that difference," Athena put in, tossing Fargo a sharp glance.

"Overloaded wagons mean trouble," Fargo said coldly. "We'll talk about it later." He moved to the next wagon, the second of the canvas-topped hay wagons, and Athena hurried to catch up to his long-legged stride. As he reached the wagon, a girl swung down to the ground in a graceful, easy motion, and he took in long legs wrapped in tight Levi's, a lithe, narrow-hipped figure with breasts under a tan shirt that curved upward in sharp, twin points. Brown hair cut short framed a pert face with a small, upturned nose and Cupid's-bow red lips. Her light-brown eyes surveyed him with something more than interest, a wariness behind the surface of her glance.

"This is Darcy Clark, Fargo," Athena introduced, and Fargo felt her take in his frank appreciation of the girl's figure.

"You traveling alone?" Fargo asked Darcy Clark.

"That's right," she said, leaned against the side of the wagon with a gesture that just edged challenge. "No law against that, is there?" she said, and the challenge was unmistakable now.

"Why?" Fargo asked gruffly.

He saw a thin veil slip over the light-brown eyes. "Maybe I just like traveling alone." She half-smiled.

"Try again," he grunted.

"I'm an artist," Darcy Clark said, an edge of disdain in her tone. "I've an assignment for a magazine back East, *Harper's Weekly*, to do a fully illustrated story on a wagon-train expedition. I work best alone. Does that explain everything to your satisfaction?" she asked with mocking amusement.

"For now," Fargo said, and watched her eyebrows arch faintly. "I just hope you can handle more than a paintbrush."

"I can," she said coolly, and Fargo turned from her. Darcy Clark was full of thorns, sheathed now, but they were there and he wondered why.

The last Conestoga waited and beside it a woman in her late thirties, perhaps forty, Fargo guessed, with a still-attractive face, blond hair with enough gray in it so that it gave her an ash-blond appearance. She wore it hanging loosely from a tie at the back of her neck. Her face just avoided being raw-boned and large, somewhat shapeless breasts filled a light-gray shirt. But her eyes held him, burning with a restless intensity, eyes that bored deeply into him with an inner turbulence.

"I'm Henrietta Crown," she said, half-turned as a man came into view. "This is my driver, Amos Alder," she said. Fargo took in the man with one sweeping glance, saw a medium-built man with plain, undistinguished features under thick, black hair.

"Howdy," the man offered, and his voice held deference. Amos Alder was a man accustomed to being deferential, Fargo decided.

"You know what you've hired yourself into, Amos?" Fargo asked.

"I've told him," Henrietta Crown answered.

"I'd like to hear Amos," Fargo said, and met the woman's intense stare.

"I know what happened to the last train at Condor Pass," the man said. "Henrietta told me when she hired me. But work's scarce out here if you're not a cowhand."

"What are you, Amos?" Fargo asked.

"Used to be a coachman back East. Came to Colorado to drive for a man who up and died. Drove a stage in the Kansas territory for a while, but that came to an end," Amos said.

Fargo brought his glance back to Henrietta Crown. Her intense stare continued to bore into him, giving her face a vibrancy it didn't really possess. "What are you doing on this expedition?" Fargo asked her.

"Going to California. I hear it's a good place and I've a cousin there. I'm tired of being alone since I lost my husband," the woman said. Her eyes shifted away, returned, restless, intense eyes fueled by some inner flame. He'd seen the likes of it in women too long without a man, yet there was something different in Henrietta Crown's intensity. He'd need more time to get a handle on it, he decided and turned as he heard the sound of hoofbeats and saw Joe Pueblo riding back. The Indian reined up a half-dozen yards distant, and Fargo strode past the semicircle of wagons toward him. Athena hurried up after him as he halted before the dark-brown gelding.

"Any problems?" Fargo asked.

"Lots of people stop to read it. I hang around and watch," Joe said.

"Good. Stretch your legs some," Fargo said, and Joe Pueblo moved away as Athena looked at the big black-haired man with a touch of disdain in her blue-green eyes.

"Satisfied with everyone's answers?" she slid at him.

"Does it matter?" he returned.

"Not really," she snapped. "I'm satisfied, and that's what counts."

The sharp sound of a horse's neigh cut off answering and he turned to see Darcy Clark hanging on to the cheek strap of a gray mare that balked at a feed bag. As the horse tossed its head high, Darcy Clark's slender form rose with it and Fargo watched one upturned breast press hard against the tan shirt, outlining a tiny point. She was about to lose her hold on the mare and the feed bag when he stepped forward, brought his hand alongside the mare's jaw, holding it there in a steady, soothing touch. The mare responded at once, growing calm as Darcy fixed the buckle on the feed-bag strap in place. Fargo continued to stroke the mare's heavy jawbone as she settled down to nose into the feed bag. Darcy stepped back and he felt her eyes moving up and down his long, hard-muscled frame.

"You looking as an artist or as a woman?" he asked without turning. When he glanced at her, he saw cool amusement veiling the light-brown eyes.

"Whichever you like," she answered, and turned away and disappeared inside the wagon. He watched her rear, tight and compact, as she vanished from sight. Darcy Clark was adding an unexpected interest to the trip, he reflected as Athena's voice cut into his thoughts sharply, too sharply. He smiled to himself.

"Fargo," she called, her voice edged. The seawater eyes had turned a brittle emerald, he saw as he ambled up to her. "I don't want any unnecessary complications," she bit out.

"Such as?" he inquired innocently.

"You know very well such as," she snapped.

"Is that a touch of jealousy?" he asked in mock surprise.

Athena's mouth fell open and her lips moved soundlessly. "It certainly is not," she hissed as she recovered her voice. "But you were hired for your talents as a trailsman not as a stud."

"You're in luck. They go together. It's a package deal." He smiled amiably, touched his hat brim, and started to walk on.

"Dammit, Fargo, I expect you to pay attention to me," she called after him.

"I will, honey. Don't you fret any about that," he tossed back.

"And stop twisting my words," she half-shouted.

He paused, threw a wide smile at her. "Am I?" he asked. She was still glaring at him as he walked on to where Joe Pueblo sat cross-legged on the ground. Fargo sat down beside the still figure, leaned back.

"Maybe we go to town soon," Joe said. Fargo studied the impassive face and let his silence voice the question. "Too many people look at sign," Joe said.

Fargo pondered for a moment. Joe Pueblo had caught hold of something in Drovers Bend, a moment or a mood, enough to voice in his oblique way, and that was more than enough for him, Fargo thought as he rose to his feet. "Let's go," he said, striding to the pinto.

He rode the short distance into Drovers Bend at a fast trot, slowed only when he reached the town's main street and started to make his way past wagons and packhorses. Joe Pueblo fell a half-pace behind him and Fargo was nearing the saloon when he saw the figure move out from beneath the overhang of a building, Ellsworth Pond's well-tailored form stepping into his path. Two men were with him, one in a stiff banker's collar and dark-blue suit, the other wearing a shopkeeper's white apron.

"Been waiting to see you, Fargo," Ellsworth Pond said as Fargo halted, stayed in the saddle. Ellsworth Pond's oversized features seemed to come together in a serious frown. "Seems you're taking that Neils girl's wagon train out," the man said grimly.

Fargo's eyes took a moment to scan the half-dozen others who had gathered behind Pond and watch four or five more stopping, two of them women with shopping baskets. "Looks that way," he said, returning his glance to Ellsworth Pond. "She's paying top dollar."

"She's crazy, you know," Pond said.

"That so?" Fargo said.

"Plumb crazy. I'm not the only one who says so," Pond went on, glancing at the others for instant approval. "The tragic death of her father unhinged the poor girl. She can't just accept what happened. She's trying to find a scapegoat."

"How?" Fargo asked mildly.

"By trying to blame me when everyone knows better than that," Pond said. "I did all I could, hired experienced outriders, saw that everybody had new wagons. I can't help it if that idiot colonel fell down on his job."

"You agree he should have picked up some signs," Fargo said.

"Of course he should have, but he didn't and she's got no right blaming me for that," Pond protested, and drew a murmur of sympathy from the others. "Yet she's hell-bent on taking another wagon train through Condor Pass. She ought to be stopped."

The murmur of sympathy became one of angry agreement. "Why?" Fargo asked.

"Hell, the Comanche have made it plain they won't let another train through Condor Pass. All she's going to do is bring on another massacre, get herself and all those folks killed. She's crazy, I tell you," Pond insisted.

"Maybe," Fargo conceded. "But she's told everyone the risks."

"Hah!" Pond grunted derisively. "She's told them with you on hand they'll get through. She's sold those poor folks a bill of goods."

Fargo half-smiled. There was truth enough in Pond's assertion. "She's got to be stopped," he heard another voice say, turned his glance on the man in the dark-blue suit. "She's going to ruin Drovers Bend," the man added. "Another massacre and we'll be known as a jinx town. Nobody'll leave from here for anywhere."

"That's right," the man wearing the white apron said. "People are superstitious and a town can get a bad name right quick. They'll avoid Drovers Bend like the plague if it gets known as a jinx town."

"And that'll be bad for business," Fargo remarked.

"Damn right," the man said to a chorus of sullen agreement.

"You're making a mistake helping her, Fargo," Pond said. "She couldn't go it without you."

Fargo allowed a slow smile. "I made an agreement. I don't go for breaking them. Maybe I can convince her it's a bad idea after we've gone a spell."

Ellsworth Pond's eyes narrowed a fraction. "It's your neck. Don't expect sympathy from anyone around here," the man said, and drew an agreeing rumble from the others.

"Wouldn't think of it," Fargo answered, touched the pinto's ribs with his heels, and the horse started forward. The small crowd parted as he rode through, Joe Pueblo following, coming up alongside him as he cleared the others.

"Town stirred up pretty good," Joe commented.

"Some for their own reasons, but Pond's had a hand in it, I'd guess," Fargo said. "How do you read him, Joe?"

"Either he very hurt fella or very worried fella," Joe Pueblo said.

Fargo's laugh was wry, Joe Pueblo's analysis both succinct and accurate. But if Pond were worried, what was he worried about? The question still made no sense. Fargo frowned, thinking of the man's cousin being one of the victims. And if he were very hurt, that meant all the strange things could be explained away as bad planning, stupidity, and carelessness, and that was too damn much to buy. The saloon came into sight and he put away thoughts to focus on the four figures lounging near the sign.

He halted the pinto, let his lake-blue eyes scan the quartet. Three were hard-mouthed, narrow-eyed, and weathered, a type he'd seen too often in too many places, drifters with a taste for trouble but not expert enough to stand up as gunfighters. The fourth one was cut from a different cloth, young, not more than twenty, he guessed, cold blue eyes and cruelty in the twist of his mouth. He looked up at the Ovaro and the big man in the saddle with casual conceit.

"I'm Fargo," the Trailsman said. "You the only four waiting?"

"Just us," the young one answered. "I guess nobody's anxious to be massacred." He smiled at his remark and the smile was made of ice.

"What makes you anxious?" Fargo asked.

The young man made a harsh sound. "I won't be massacred. I shoot too fast and too straight," he said, his tone full of cockiness.

"And you enjoy killing," Fargo remarked.

"That's right," the man said. "This sounds like the chance to get paid for some good target practice."

"What's your name?" Fargo asked.

"Denny, Bud Denny," the young man said. "Want to see a shootin' sample?"

"Another time," Fargo said, and saw Denny's young face show disappointment. He turned his attention to the others, who formed a half-circle. "You three together?" he asked.

"Been travelin' together for a while," the one man answered, a wiry-built man with a worn shirt. "I'm Hawkins. This here is Broadman and that's Smith," he said, gesturing to the others. "We've done outriding. We know how to keep a sharp eye."

"That's good enough for me," Fargo said.

"What about the pay?" Broadman asked.

"Three dollars a day, twenty-five percent more when it's over," Fargo said, and the men nodded agreement at once. "There's a house just north of town. You'll see the wagons around it. Be there one hour after daylight," he said.

"We'll be there," Bud Denny said in an almost bored voice, and Fargo wheeled the pinto around and started back through town. Joe Pueblo moved up beside him, cast an expressionless glance at him.

"They'll do for what you want of them," Joe commented.

"What's that?" Fargo returned evenly.

"To use up Comanche arrows," Joe grunted, drew a thin smile from the big black-haired man.

"You know me too well," Fargo said.

"I know you wouldn't hire those coyotes for anything else," Joe said. The remark didn't need an answer and Fargo stayed silent as he rode back through Drovers Bend, caught a few angry stares from merchants in the doorways of their stores. Darkness began to settle itself as he reached the semicircle of wagons and dismounted. Joe Pueblo swung down with him, tethered his horse beside Fargo's gleaming black-and-white Ovaro.

Henrietta Crown had taken cooking duties and she dished out tin plates from beside a steaming iron kettle over a small fire. Fargo returned Herb Atkinson's greeting as he walked toward Henrietta behind Joe Pueblo, watched the woman stare intensely at Joe as she filled his plate with a good-smelling stew, and he saw the woman's eyes follow Joe as he walked away with his plate. Fargo stepped forward, held out his plate, and Henrietta Crown's eyes returned to glance quickly at him as she began to dish out the stew. The firelight smoothed the heavier planes of her face, turned her gray-blond hair a silvery tone, and she seemed almost handsome. But it also made her intense brown eyes seem even stronger. He saw the line of her jaw tighten as she glanced to where Joe had sat down with his plate.

"He going with us?" she asked Fargo as she emptied another ladle of stew onto the tin plate.

"He is," Fargo said, saw the tightness come into her lips. "That bothers you," he remarked.

"Guess so," she murmured, looking down.

"Because he's an Indian," Fargo probed.

"Yes," she said darkly.

"Thanks for being honest," Fargo said. "He's a good man. You'll be glad he's along."

"You, maybe, not me," Henrietta Crown said. "But I'll have to live with it." She lifted her head, her eyes probing into Fargo. He wondered again about her eyes. Something pent up behind them. Hungers too long denied? Again he had to halt at accepting that. Something else, he murmured inwardly, but something.

He took his plate, ate quickly, and had finished when Athena stepped from her wagon and came over to him. "Did you get your outriders?" she asked briskly.

"We pull out after dawn tomorrow." He nodded and saw satisfaction touch her face.

She called out to the others at once. "We move first thing, come morning. Everyone get a good night's sleep," she ordered, tossed Fargo a curt nod, and hurried into her wagon. He brought his empty plate to where Mary Atkinson cleaned and dried the tinware beside a water barrel. She allowed a small smile, as held in as the rest of her face, and Fargo moved to halt at the Reverend Moreland's wagon, his eyes fastening on the end of the pump organ. He was still frowning at it in thought when Judith Moreland appeared, her plump face scrubbed and shining, towel and hard soap in her hand and a flannel nightdress cloaking her plump figure.

"Worry not, Mister Fargo," she said airily. "My little pump organ will be a source of joy, not trouble."

"Will it, now?" he growled. "I figure you've a ramp to get it in and out of the wagon."

"Yes, it's on rollers and it moves easily. It's not all that heavy," she said.

"You're still overloaded," he said.

Her round face clouded with alarm. "You're not going to make me leave it here, are you?" she asked.

Fargo looked at the square, thick shape in the wagon for a moment, returned his eyes to Judith Moreland. "Wouldn't think of it," he said affably, and saw her face wreath itself in delight.

"You are a good man, Mister Fargo. I knew it," she said.

"The best," he agreed as he walked on to where the pinto was tethered. He took his bedroll down, laid it on the ground a few yards outside the semicircle of wagons. Joe Pueblo had disappeared with his blanket into the outer darkness. He'd bed down alone, on the perimeter of camp. It was his way, except in special instances, and Fargo smoothed his bedroll, stepped to the wagons to take another glance at the half-circle. He saw Mary Atkinson being helped inside by her husband and noted that Amos Alder had bedded down *under* Henrietta's wagon.

He started past Athena's Conestoga and halted. She'd a kerosene lamp lighted inside and her shadow was sharply outlined against the canvas of the wagon top. As he watched, she lifted her arms, her body clearly silhouetted, and he saw she had nothing on as she slowly turned first one way, then the other. She was moving her body in a series of limbering-up exercises, her rounded breasts lifting, swaying, still no sign of tiny points on the sharply etched outline. She half-rose, stretched her legs backward, and executed a variation of a push-up. She had a lovely little rear, he noted, rounder and fuller than it appeared under clothes, and he watched it move up and down until she halted, swung herself around to a sitting position. She pulled her arms backward, thrust her breasts out, moved her torso back and forth to perform a silhouetted little sitting ballet. He watched until she finished, saw her stretch out on what was obviously a mattress. "Very nice," he said softly but clearly.

The silhouetted figure snapped upright, pulled a robe on, and seconds later Athena pushed her head outside the canvas top.

"Did you know that a lamp throws a perfect silhouette against canvas?" Fargo asked brightly.

"And it would have been too much to expect you to look the other way," she bit out.

"Now, why would I do that?" Fargo asked.

"It's called being a gentleman," she snapped.

"It's called being a damn fool." Fargo smiled.

"Well, you'll not have to concern yourself about that, again," she sniffed, pulled her head back in, and the lamp went dark.

Fargo smiled as he moved on, had taken only a few strides when he heard the laugh, soft and velvety. He halted, peered at the wagon, saw it was Darcy Clark's as the slender form stepped into view. She wore a pink housedress held together only with a matching belt.

"I couldn't help overhearing. I was getting a breath of night air," Darcy Clark said. She leaned back against a wheel of the wagon and her breasts pressed against the thin material, a saucy, upward line to their shape, ending in twin dots. "Our Athena Neils is a bit stuffy, I'd say," Darcy Clark commented.

"Maybe," Fargo said. "But then maybe she's just wound up tight. She's very serious about this venture."

"Yes, isn't she?" Darcy said. "It's really all rather ridiculous."

Fargo picked up the edge of bitchiness in Darcy Clark's tone. "How do you mean that?" he asked casually.

"All this trying to prove the last wagon train wasn't

run properly. She's made no secret of that," the girl said. "I really don't know what she's so bothered over, but it all seems rather unnecessary and pointless."

Once again the edge was in the girl's tone. "Might be," Fargo agreed, saw Darcy Clark's light-brown eyes studying him.

"I'm surprised a man like you had gone along with her in this," she remarked.

"I've gone along with the money she offered," Fargo said blandly, and saw the moment of satisfaction touch Darcy's eyes.

"That I can understand." She smiled, a sudden burst of warmth that made her pert prettiness soften. "Good night, Fargo," she said abruptly, swung up on the wagon. The pink housedress opened enough to reveal a glimpse of a long, lithe, beautifully shaped leg with a delicious little round knee. She disappeared into the wagon and Fargo went to his bedroll, settled down to sleep thinking about the note of disdain Darcy had in her tone when she spoke of Athena. Just bitchiness, or that female intuition that cuts through to the heart of things? he pondered. He fell asleep, still turning the question in his mind, and the semicircle of wagons grew silent under a sky of low flying clouds.

He'd slept for some hours when he woke, the sound insistent in his ears, the soft, quavering, trilled call of the yellow warbler. His eyes came open and he listened. The call came again, rolling across the silence, definitely the yellow warbler. Fargo's hand stole to the big Colt .45 at his side. No yellow warbler, not here and not at this hour, not by a damn sight. Joe Pueblo, he murmured silently as the call came again, and Fargo eased himself up on one elbow, his eyes sweeping the darkness. He saw the figures, then, one nearest him just bending under Athena's wagon, two more almost at the reverend's Conestoga, a fourth one creeping bent over toward the Atkinson wagon.

Each of the figures carried something and Fargo squinted through the night as he silently lifted himself to one knee. Buckets, he muttered, they were carrying buckets. Frowning, he saw the nearest figure crawling under the front of Athena's wagon, watched the man pour the contents of the bucket onto the underside of the wagon. Out of the corner of his eye, Fargo saw Joe Pueblo moving down toward the wagons as the other men started to pour their buckets over the wagon carriages. On his feet, the Colt in one hand, his finger resting on the trigger, Fargo moved quickly, long, silent strides putting him at the first wagon in seconds. The man, still under the wagon, half-turned, felt the figure coming at him, and his eyes widened in surprise.

"Come out slow," Fargo growled, raising the Colt.

The man paused for an instant, flung himself sideways. He yelled out as he hit the ground in front of the wagon and his hand yanked at his gun. "*Run!*" he screamed as he tried to fire from half on his back. Fargo's gun resounded in the night and the man's body arched backward to smash against the spokes of the nearest wheel. Fargo saw the others dashing from beneath the wagons, guns drawn, and he saw Joe Pueblo flatten himself on the ground as two of the figures sent a volley of bullets at him. Fargo took aim, fired, as one of the men started to spin his way. The shot tore into the figure and the man continued to spin, twisting completely around, then half around again before pitching to the ground.

The third figure streaked, crouched over, to a quartet of horses in the distance, and Fargo saw Joe Pueblo, moving close to the ground, coming in to cut him off; then he glimpsed the fourth man, saw a sudden flare of light in his hand. As a silent oath formed inside him, Fargo saw the match sail through the air, a tiny arc of light that landed beneath the Atkinson wagon. The match lay there, flamed for a suspended second, and as if by magic, the underside of the wagon erupted into flame. Fargo, on a dead run for the wagon, fired a shot at the fleeing figure and had the satisfaction of seeing the man's head seem to disappear, the rest of his body hurtling forward with the reflex actions of a beheaded chicken before crumpling to the ground.

He reached the wagon as Herb Atkinson leaped from it, pulling his wife after him, both clutching blankets. The flames ran up and down the undercarriage at the front of the wagon, two tongues of fire curling around the wheels. Others, awake now, recovered from initial surprise and rushed forward with blankets, beating at the flames as Fargo tore the cover from the water barrel and tossed the contents onto the underside of the wagon. A sizable section of flame hissed away in a cloud of black, sharp smoke and the others managed to beat out the rest with blankets.

Fargo sniffed the air again, his lips drawn back. "Kerosene," he bit out, his eyes taking in the still-shocked faces gathered before him. Athena pushed forward, the robe around her, and he saw that Darcy Clark, the pink housedress hardly closed, looked on with incomprehension on her pert face.

"We had company," Fargo said, gesturing to the silent figures sprawled nearby. "Joe Pueblo saw them first."

"They were trying to set the wagons on fire?" Abe Sprain asked incredulously.

"With buckets of kerosene. They doused three other wagons, but only one had a chance to light his." He saw everyone shoot a glance at their wagons. "The air will evaporate it by morning," Fargo told them reassuringly as Joe Pueblo appeared. "Yours get away?" Fargo asked.

"No, but he won't be answering anything," Joe said, and looked apologetic. Fargo nodded, remembering how accurate Joe was with his hunting knife.

"Who and why?" Athena spoke up.

"I don't know who but I know why. No wagons, no wagon train into Condor Pass," Fargo said.

"Ellsworth Pond," Athena said almost triumphantly.

"Maybe not," Fargo said.

"What do you mean?" She frowned in protest.

"He says he did all anyone could do last time. He claims that idiot colonel he hired fell down on the job," Fargo said.

"Pond said that?" Darcy Clark cut in.

"Exactly," Fargo answered.

"That bastard," Darcy hissed, and Fargo felt his brows lift in surprise as he turned to her. She half-shrugged and wiped anger from her face. "It's not that I care. I just think that's a rotten thing to say," Darcy explained. "The man was massacred. He's not here to defend himself and Pond has no right to go around slandering people." She paused, met Fargo's appraising stare. "A sense of fair play, it's called. I've always had it," she said.

"Good enough," he said as Athena's voice interrupted.

"Who but Pond would have tried this?" she asked.

"The good merchants of Drovers Bend. They're plenty stirred up. They're afraid you're risking another massacre that will make Drovers Bend into a jinx town. They could've hired those four to torch your wagons," Fargo told her.

"It's over and it doesn't matter much now," Jeff Howard put in sensibly. "We'll be on our way in a few hours. I suggest we all finish getting some sleep."

He started back to his wagon, Abe Sprain following, and Fargo saw the Reverend Moreland, holding himself inside a black coat, glance at the still forms on the ground. "Are you going to do the proper thing with those men, Fargo?" he asked. Judith peered past her brother's shoulder, her round face wide-eyed.

"Yes, sir," Fargo said. "I'm going to put them on their horses and send them back to town."

Reverend Moreland paused, decided not to press the matter. He turned away and the others began to drift off with slow sober steps. All except Darcy, Fargo observed. She returned to her wagon with a brisk, impatient stride, the pink housedress clinging to the long line of her legs. Athena hung back a moment, her eyes searching the big black-haired man's strong face.

"Don't you see what this proves?" she said. "It shows that Pond's afraid of what I'll find out."

"I see it doesn't prove a damn thing. We don't know who was behind it and so it's just one more question mark for now," Fargo threw back.

She glowered at him for a moment and then stalked to her wagon to disappear inside. Fargo turned to where Joe Pueblo waited.

"She see what she wants to see in everything, that one," Joe commented.

"It's called being blind sure," Fargo growled. "Come on, give me a hand."

A few minutes later four horses were sent trotting down the road toward town with their silent riders bent over, each strapped to their saddle horns.

"Somebody will get an answer," Fargo muttered as Joe trudged into the darkness and his blanket. Fargo lay down on his bedroll as irritation swept over him. Four dead men and no proof of anything. Waste, a total waste all around, and he disliked waste. All that had come out of it was that Darcy Clark had a strong sense of fair play. He turned on his side and slept quickly. He'd be damned if he'd waste the remaining few hours till dawn in pointless speculation.

4

Bud Denny and the other three arrived promptly, Fargo noted in satisfaction as the morning sun was but an hour old. He introduced the four men to everyone. Bud Denny's cold, arrogant eyes took in Athena with a casual glance and went on to linger on Darcy. He couldn't blame the man, Fargo commented silently. Athena's white blouse was coolly businesslike, with stupidly long sleeves and a high collar. Darcy had taken a deep-red shirt and tucked it up and under. It formed a bare midriff that revealed a beautifully tanned, narrow waist while it cradled the sharp, upturned breasts that pushed against the material.

"Joe Pueblo will give you your flanking positions," Fargo said.

The man's mouth tightened, a cruel twist to it, as he turned his eyes on Fargo. "You didn't say I'd be taking orders from an Indian," he growled.

"I didn't say a lot of things. You quit now or ride with him. Your decision, sonny," Fargo said.

Bud Denny's temper flared instantly. "Don't call me sonny, mister," he barked.

"Then act like a man," Fargo said calmly, met Bud Denny's angry eyes with quiet firmness. The man's young face stayed angry as he wheeled his horse and followed Joe Pueblo out past the wagons.

"I don't like him," Athena said. "But he did back down."

Fargo made a harsh sound. "He backed away, not down. There's a difference."

Athena peered at him, the seawater eyes turning cool blue. "Why did you do such a turnaround on the pump organ?" she asked suspiciously. "Judith told me you were positively pleasant. She's convinced you're really a wonderful fellow."

"I am." Fargo grinned at her.

"Why the sudden change-about?" she pressed.

"You know, you've a suspicious nature, Athena," he told her.

"Where some people are concerned," she snapped.

"And you're going to sweat yourself out in that blouse," he commented, gave her a glance of pained tolerance. "Athena . . . what the hell kind of a name is that, anyway?" He frowned.

"An ancient Greek name. I told you my father was a professor of anthropology. Athena was the Greek goddess of battle," she answered.

Fargo gave a harsh grunt. "You might just have the right name, after all. Let's hope she's on our side," he said, waved his arm into the air, and sent the wagons moving forward. He rode out in front of Athena's wagon, turned to the side, let the others roll past. The Reverend Moreland's Conestoga creaked as the overloaded axles turned; Fargo's mouth tightened for a moment. The six extra horses, reined together, followed along after the last of the wagons, Abe Sprain and Jeff Howard sitting together on the driver's seat. Fargo sent the pinto cantering on ahead, moved into the flat country, and his eyes checked on the positions of his outriders. Joe Pueblo had disappeared and Fargo moved forward, spotted Joe in the distance. The trail stayed close to a long line of sandstone buttresses on the right, the broad, mostly flat land spreading out on the left.

Fargo settled the pinto into a leisurely pace, relaxed in the saddle. Only his eyes, sweeping back and forth, revealed that he wasn't out on a casual pleasure ride. He called a rest halt at noon, when the sun was burning high and hot, picked a shady place beside the sandstone where a trickle of water inched along the rocks.

Bud Denny and the other outriders drew in, dismounted, and stretched out in the shade.

Fargo tossed Athena a smile as he passed her. She had rolled up her sleeves, unbuttoned the high collar of the blouse, and patted water onto her face. She answered his smile with a small glare.

He halted at Darcy where she sat against a rock, relaxing. His glance went to the line of magenta flowers that stretched alongside the sandstone, brilliant against their long, green, vinelike stems. They formed a slash of brilliance across the dry terrain. "Beautiful, aren't they?" he said admiringly. "Red-tail cactus. You don't come across them often, especially in flower."

"Yes, they are gorgeous," Darcy remarked, her eyes moving up to him as he peered down at her. He studied her for another moment. "You're thinking something," she said with the hint of a smile.

"Nothing that needs saying now," he answered.

"You still surprised at what I said about fair play last night?" she probed.

"Yes," he said, deciding to let her run with that thought.

"I took you for a man who thinks the same way," Darcy said.

"You're right," Fargo remarked.

A note of satisfaction passed her eyes. "That's good to hear," she said. Her sudden smile came, full of warmth. "You know, I really feel quite alone sometimes on this trip. I think I'm more than a little nervous."

"You asking me to pay special attention to you?" Fargo slid back.

Her eyes grew sly and soft, "Something like that," she said.

"I'll work on it," he said, and a slightly smug expression touched her face as he walked back to the pinto. He turned the conversation with Darcy in his mind. It had been made of half-truths. She wanted special attention but not just for the reasons she'd tossed out. Darcy Clark was playing games. But what kind and why? he mused as he leaned against a sandstone wall. His eyes moved over the wagons, paused at Henrietta Crown. The woman stood alone, her intense, restless eyes staring out across the flatland. Henrietta Crown was a half-truth, too, cloaking something devouring behind that strong face. His eyes swung back to Darcy, narrowed in thought as he watched her continue to relax. One at a time and he'd start with Darcy, he muttered inwardly.

He gave them another half-hour, then moved the wagons forward again. Athena kept her sleeves rolled up and collar unbuttoned. She'd pulled her hair back, secured it with a bright-blue ribbon. It showed the graceful curve of her neck and Athena saw him watching her as she passed in front of him.

"I like it," he commented idly.

"It was done for comfort, not appearance, I assure you," she said.

"Didn't figure anything else," he commented, and watched her sit stiffly straight as she drove on. He watched Bud Denny ride alongside Darcy for a few minutes before peeling off to take up his flanking position along with Smith and Broadman. Joe Pueblo was already a distance away, his horse moving almost aimlessly. Judith Moreland held the reins as the reverend passed with an expansive nod. Amos Alder drove, Henrietta sitting beside him. Her large breasts swayed loosely to the roll of the wagon and her gray-blond hair, blending together in the strong sun, gave her a mature, overflowing earth-mother sensuality.

Mary Atkinson sat beside Herb on their wagon, hands folded demurely in her lap, her face quietly composed. She looked, Fargo thought, as though she were on her way to a Sunday church service. But then, Mary Atkinson always looked that way, he decided, probably in bed, too. Though he wouldn't take bets on that. He'd been fooled by proper, demure faces, he reflected with fond memories and the edge of a smile touched his lips as he turned the pinto and rode on ahead. He left the wagons behind and carefully scanned the sandstone pillars as he rode, espied a passageway, and steered the pinto up into the narrow opening. He rode slowly, his eyes scanning the ground and the rock, testing, probing, making a series of explorations into smaller side passages. Finally satisfied, he drifted down again to where the line of wagons moved steadily westward.

Darcy had draped the reins over the rail of her seat, let the team go on by itself, rode with her eyes half-closed, her face lifted to the sun. Fargo watched her for a moment, and with his eyes narrowed in thought, he rode on to where Joe Pueblo had slowed almost to a halt. Joe nodded to a distant line of gray purple on the horizon, the harbinger of dusk crawling its way toward them. Fargo signified agreement and motioned the wagons into a wide opening in a series of loose-jointed, high, conical rock formations. He'd allow a good hour to cook and settle in before night arrived. As they grew into a trail routine, he'd cut down on the time needed to set up camp.

The wagons maneuvered into a semicircle. Mary had drawn cooking chores, he saw. The approaching dusk, still tinted with the last of the sun, laid a delicate lavender carpet across the flatland and turned the sandstone rocks into deep-purple castles. He watched the spectacular beauty of it and noticed Henrietta pause nearby to stare across the open space. Something close to fear pulled her face tight and she flicked a quick restless glance at him.

"Nothing out there now," he said gently.

The woman drew a deep breath that all but burst her heavy breasts through the top of the dress. "The night's out there and I hate the night," she said.

"Too many dreams?" he asked.

Her intense eyes bored into him. "Too many," she muttered, and walked away quickly as his frown followed her. Maybe he'd been right in the first place, he reflected, inner hungers too long held back. They'd be harder to live with in the deep of the night. Whatever it was, it burned hard inside her. He turned from the delicate beauty of the surroundings, saw Darcy as she sat at the rear of her wagon, intent on cleaning trail dust from her boots.

Joe Pueblo rode up and dropped the gelding's rains over a harness shaft. He strolled beside Fargo to where Mary had the food readied. They ate in silence and Fargo waited till everyone had finished before standing. "We start posting sentries tonight," he announced. "Joe Pueblo will set up a rotation schedule. Four-hour shifts."

"You saw signs of the Comanche," Athena said at once.

"No," Fargo said curtly, irritated at her tone of eagerness when there should have been alarm.

"No?" she echoed, her face falling. He wasn't the only one who'd caught her tone, he saw as Darcy's voice cut in, an acid sweetness in it.

"You sound almost disappointed, Athena," she remarked. "I mean, I should think you'd be quite happy there aren't any Comanche signs."

Fargo saw Athena's eyes slide into a dark green. "Of course I am," she said. "I just want to know why the sentries, then."

"I don't like surprises," Fargo answered.

Athena tossed him a glance of wary acceptance, returned her eyes to Darcy. "I don't need you to interpret my reactions, if you don't mind," Athena slid out coldly. "I'm running this wagon train and I'll question anything and everything I wish to question."

Darcy's lips tightened and she turned away, her eyes flashing as she saw the amused smile that had come to touch the big black-haired man's face. Fargo started to walk away when Reverend Moreland's voice boomed out.

"We'll be having evening prayer services, Brother Fargo. You'll be staying, won't you?" the minister said, turning the invitation into a subtle reproach.

"You stand in for me tonight, Reverend," Fargo called back as he kept walking into the darkness beyond the flickering firelight's reach. As he unsaddled the pinto, he watched the reverend and Judith lower the small ramp from the end of the Conestoga and roll the pump organ down. Minutes later, Judith sat at the keyboard on a small stool, pumped the pedals, and the organ began to sound, the notes of a hymn taking shape. Fargo made a mental note that it had taken only a half-minute to roll the organ from the wagon.

He took the rubber curry from his saddlebag and began to give the pinto a quick grooming, watched the others gather around the organ as Judith led the hymn singing. All except Bud Denny, who watched from a distance, and Darcy, who stayed in her wagon. The reverend ended the service with a short prayer and he and Judith rolled the organ back into the Conestoga. Minutes later, the fire was out and the wagons settling into quietness. Joe had put Herb Atkinson and Jeff Howard out for the first four-hour sentry shift, Fargo saw as the men took up their posts. He watched Joe's figure disappear into the darkness beyond and he took his bedroll, started toward the sandstone pillars when he saw Darcy step from her wagon. She began to walk out into the warm night and he watched her for a moment, then stepped after her.

"Get back," he said softly, and she spun in surprise. "No strolls," he said. "Not tonight, not any night."

"I can't sleep," she said crossly.

"You asked for it," Fargo said mildly.

Darcy's light-brown eyes caught a glint of inner fire. "Well, the way she said it just bothered me," Darcy returned, anger touching her voice. "She's got an obsession about proving the first train wasn't run right. It's ridiculous, really."

"Maybe," Fargo said.

Darcy frowned. "Meaning what?" she snapped. "You saying you go along with her obsession?"

"I'm saying maybe, that's all, just maybe," Fargo answered.

Darcy stared into the distance. "I still can't sleep yet," she said. "Can we talk some?"

"You want some of that special attention?" he asked.

She half-shrugged. "I guess maybe," she said.

"I'm going to get ready to sleep. You can come watch if you want," he told her. She met his eyes but didn't back any. He started to go up a narrow path in the sandstone and she fell into step beside him.

"I understand the Comanche don't leave any signs," she said as they climbed.

"They leave signs. They're not made of air. You just have to know their ways and how to look and where to look," Fargo said.

She lapsed into silence, obviously turning his answer in her mind as he halted at a secluded little spot, a nest-like circle inside the sandstone that still held the heat of the day. He spread out the bedroll, put the Colt in its holster on the ground at the edge of the blanket, pulled off shirt and trousers, and stretched out in his shorts. Darcy, her back to him, sat with her knees drawn up to her chin and he smiled as he saw her slide little glances at his beautifully muscled form.

"Talk," he said, and she didn't reply. Suddenly her pert face, the short hair, and her drawn-together position made her seem very small and very alone. He reached out, put a hand on her shoulder, gently pulled. She came around to face him. "No talk?" he asked.

She shook her head, the short-cut hair bouncing from side to side, and he saw her tongue touch the edge of her upper lip. His hand on her shoulder increased its pressure and she came forward, her Cupid's-bow mouth opening. Her hand moved, rested against his abdomen for a moment.

"Oh, God," she breathed, but her hand stayed, pressed, slid upward onto his chest. He brought her head to his, her lips to his mouth, let his tongue slip forward against them. She gave a tiny shudder and her gasp answered him as he pressed her mouth open. His tongue reached in, warm sweet wetness, and he felt her hands tighten against him. His fingers undid the buttons on the red shirt and the material fell open as he pulled her down onto the bedroll. The blouse fell from her shoulders as he pushed gently and her breasts turned upward to him, not terribly large but saucy, curving beautifully to sharp little rosy tips. His hand curled around one, his thumb tracing a circle over the dusty-pink areola.

Her breath drew in with a long gasp and he felt her legs lifting, hands pushing down, and then she lay naked beside him, narrow-hipped, a flat stomach, and below, a flat nap, curly and more wide than full, stretching out to the tiny folds that touched her thighs. He drew his hand down over it slowly, gently, exploring.

"Ooooh, oh, God," Darcy murmured, and he saw her legs, beautifully thin and gently curved, lift, then fall apart as though they were long, thin flower stems. Her mouth opened, pulled on his, and now her tongue began to answer, to dart forward wildly. His hand slipped lower, touched the softness of other lips, found the tiny pulsating edge.

"Iiiiiieeeee," Darcy half-screamed, and her hips thrust upward with a shuddering motion.

He touched again, drew his fingers slowly across her quivering surfaces. "Iiiiiiaaaaah . . ." she cried out again, and her hands pushed into him. He pressed deeper, slowly, probing into the soft dark of her, and he heard her breath grow deep, sounds suddenly drawn from the pit of her stomach. "Fargo, ah, ah, aaaaah . . . oh, Fargo," she managed. Her arms came around his back, pulling at him, and he moved over her, felt her long thin legs rise up, press into his sides. Her hips rose, seeking, asking, offering, and he slid into her slowly, inching his way.

"Jesus, oh, oh, my God, Fargo . . . Fargo . . ." she murmured against him. Her mouth sought his, clasped hungrily over his lips, her tongue now quivering inside him. He moved forward again, sliding deep into her, and her mouth tore from his, her head arching backward. His lips found the sharp rose tips of her breasts, pulled on their hard softness, and he felt her hips begin to lift with him, drawing upward and pushing down, in time with his very slow thrusts. Little sounds came from her, tiny murmurings of ecstasy. The sounds grew stronger, became short gasps, each one in rhythm, increasing, spiraling. Darcy's head turned from side to side and her mouth stayed open as she gasped out the sounds. Her hands pressed into his shoulders as his lips held her breast. "Oh . . . oh, God," he heard her suddenly call out, and he felt her hands become little fists against him. Her hips seemed to leap upward and the explosion was a sudden wildness, intense shuddering movements as once again her head arched backward. She clung to him as she quivered against him, holding him to her, flesh tight against flesh, and just as suddenly she fell away, deep gasping breaths escaping her.

"Too quick, too quick," she murmured, the words a half-sob. He drew from her, watched her pull her legs up as she turned on her side, face pressed into his chest. The saucy firm breasts stayed turned beautifully upward, the tiny rose tips remaining erect. "My fault," he heard her murmur. "Dammit, my fault."

He turned her on her back and the light-brown eyes stared at him as though from far away. "Nobody's fault," he said gently. "Sometimes it all gets away from you, like a horse taking the bit in its mouth."

"Can I try again tomorrow night?" she asked.

"Maybe," he said.

She snuggled against him, her arms encircling him until finally she pulled back, sat up, her breasts standing high and firm. The tiny nipples were always erect, he decided, watched her pull her blouse on, finish dressing. He stood with her and she pressed herself to him. "I'm glad I came up here with you," she said.

"You wanted to come," he remarked.

Her pert face stayed serious as she looked up at him. "I guess so," she muttered.

"Anything else you want to tell me?" Fargo asked mildly.

"Such as?" she asked, a furrow touching her brow.

He shrugged. "I don't know. Anything."

"Watch over me, Fargo," she said, reached up, brushed his lips with hers, and was hurrying away in moments. He watched her tight little rear disappear down the path, his eyes narrowed, waited till she was out of earshot, and then stretched out on the bedroll. She could reach a person with her combination of pert sauciness and little-girl lostness. That part of her was real enough, as real as her cries of pleasure had been. But another part of Darcy Clark continued to play games. He was growing more convinced of it and he decided to give himself just a little more time to be certain before calling her hand. Meanwhile, he'd enjoy as much of Darcy as he could. Somehow, he had the feeling that it might end suddenly.

He slept at once, to wake only as the sun crept over the sandstone wall. Coffee was ready when he came down to the wagons, Amos Alder serving it out of the big white enameled coffeepot. Joe Pueblo was already saddled up, he noted, as Bud Denny and Smith lounged nearby.

"See you later," Joe said to Fargo as he started out.

But Denny straightened himself, his cold eyes taking on a challenge again. "How come that Indian gets to ride out wherever he wants by himself?" the man muttered. "I'd like doin' that more than riding flanker."

"Because he's forgotten more about reading signs than you'll ever know," Fargo said pleasantly.

Bud Denny's mouth took on an arrogant twist. "But not more about fast shooting," he said. "You ready to see a sample yet?"

"In time," Fargo said evenly. "Saddle up. We're pulling out in a few minutes."

Bud Denny swaggered away with Smith, and Fargo saw Athena watching.

"He's spoiling for trouble," she said to Fargo, her glance following the younger man.

"There'll be enough to go around," Fargo remarked, and drew a thoughtful glance from her. He took in her outfit slowly and nodded approvingly at the short-sleeved shirt of light cotton she'd put on, her eyes picking up the blue of its color. "Better," he remarked.

"You know, I really didn't hire you to approve of my clothes," she said icily.

"No charge." He smiled. "Another part of the package." Her lips tightened as she turned away and clambered onto her wagon. He saddled the pinto and waved the wagons forward, Athena's in the lead. His eyes swept the flatland as they headed out, saw Hawkins and Denny riding right flank, Smith and Broadman swinging in on the left. He motioned them to spread out more and swung the pinto alongside Darcy. Her smile was full of private comments and he noted the tan shirt she wore pressed lightly against tiny twin points. They did stay erect all the time, he murmured to himself, and he dropped back to let the other wagons move up. Amos drove, Henrietta Crown beside him. She'd changed to a dress with a square-cut neckline and her large breasts ballooned out at the top.

" 'Morning, Fargo," the woman said, held him with her intense eyes. "Tell me, how long will it be before we reach Condor Pass?" she asked.

"With no delays, maybe a week," he offered, saw her eyes grow even darker. "That keeping you awake nights, too?" he prodded.

The deep burning eyes returned to him. "Some," she said. "Though Athena says there's no need to fear this time, not with you along." She paused, peered hard at him. "You agree with that?"

"No," he said flatly.

"You saying Athena Neils has been less than honest with us?" the woman asked, her tone suddenly heavy with sarcasm.

"Maybe with herself, too," Fargo said.

Henrietta Crown considered his words for a moment. "Maybe," she said slowly, almost sadly. "Doesn't much matter, anyway."

She looked at him, her eyes dark and brooding. It seemed as though those eyes were always on the verge of asking something more and then pulling back. He watched the wagon move on and Henrietta turn to staring across the flatland, drawn into herself, as though she'd pulled a shawl around her shoulders. He veered off and cantered on. The land was still, nothing moving except for pocket mice and collared lizards who seemed to conduct a contrasting dance of frantic scurrying and slow, measured motion. He kept the wagons going through the day except for short water breaks, and they had made good time when night fell. He camped at the edge of the high rock formations again, but the flatland was beginning to change shape, starting to rise and dip in the last of the dusk. Fargo stood beside the pinto and peered westward, where he could dimly make out the high ridges that mounted upward in long flat steps. At the end of their upward path, still too far away to see, Condor Pass waited. Condor Pass . . . and what else? he asked silently.

Joe Pueblo rode into camp and swung to the ground beside the big black-haired man. "Nothing," he muttered. "Too much nothing."

Fargo's smile was tight, made of grim understanding. Darcy passed on her way to the cookpot and spoke to him with her eyes. She sat down to eat with Abe Sprain and Jeff Howard and Fargo took a plate of red beans and pork fat, ate quickly, and carried his bedroll up into the rocks before the reverend began his evening prayer service. He stretched out and listened to the sound of Judith as she lead the hymn singing. It was a nice sound, he admitted, full of the strength of people standing together. For their sake, he hoped they'd have a nice, peaceful hymn sing every evening. He'd not bank on it, though, he added in grim silence.

He undressed to his shorts as the sounds from below ended and he hadn't long to wait before he heard the soft scrape of footsteps. "Over here," he called from behind the flat stone where he lay. Darcy came into sight moments later, her eyes sweeping across his near-naked form. She stepped to him, her lips parted, sank down to her knees beside him. He saw her swallow hard as she reached out, moved her hand along his chest, down over the flat hardness of his abdomen.

"Last night," she breathed, "I kept thinking about it all day."

He reached out, unbuttoned her shirt, pushed it from her, and the modest breasts curved upward to their tiny, erect dusty-pink tips. Her breath drew inside her as she came forward, pressed her breasts across his chest as he slid the rest of her clothes from her. He felt her hand on his abdomen move again, reach lower, push away his shorts, close over the pulsating maleness of him. "Ah . . . ah, God," Darcy breathed, turned onto her back, and pulled him atop her. "Please, oh, please," she pleaded. "Quick . . . quick," she cried out, and he felt her beginning to quiver. He thrust into her and she pressed her mouth into his chest and he drew backward. "No, oh, no," she protested, clutched at him, tried to pull him into her deeper. He held back and her quivering receded, became a tremored waiting.

"Easy this time, easy," he murmured against her cheek, and felt her nod as she remembered. He moved forward slowly, almost a soothing motion, back and forth, sometimes hardly moving at all.

"Yes . . . oh, oh . . . oh, yes," Darcy breathed, and this time the gathering came slowly, building itself, swelling into the eruption that finally came but only when she was ready for it, ready to savor the overwhelming sweetness of it. This time the fleeting ecstasy unleashed itself with concentrated drive and Darcy's hands pulled him to her as she writhed, clinging, crying out, clutching at every last moment of pleasure until she sank down with him and her breath seemed one long, endless sigh.

"Better this time?" Fargo asked into her ear.

"Oh, yes, oh, my God, yes," Darcy breathed, and lay against him, the erect nipples tiny soft spears pressing into his chest. He held her until she finally pushed herself up to a sitting position and reached for her shirt.

He watched her pull on clothes, and when she finished, she pressed her arms to him again. In her smile there was something more than satisfaction, almost a smugness. "You and I, Fargo, we'll make this trip something to remember," she said.

"We will," he agreed. Darcy kissed him quickly and he lay on his side watching as she left, vanishing around the edge of rock. Darcy wanted more than the pleasures of the body, he mused as he lay back. She wanted to establish a closeness with him. Once again he wondered why and felt the stab of irritation. He didn't take to being conned, not even in the best of all possible ways. He'd give Darcy another day, he growled as he drew sleep around himself. There was always the chance that he was wrong, but that chance was growing slimmer and slimmer.

The edge was still on him when morning came and he started the wagons out; Darcy's smile at him was satisfied and smug and she missed the hardness in his eyes. Overconfidence dulls the senses, he commented inwardly and became aware of Athena studying him. He drew alongside her wagon and met her speculative glance. She wore the light-blue shirt that tinted her eyes a soft aqua. "What's pushing at you this morning?" she commented.

"You'll know when I know," he snapped as Bud Denny rode up, his young face sullen.

"Let the Indian ride flank today," he said.

"I answered that yesterday. Don't push me, sonny," Fargo said.

Bud Denny's mouth took on an added twist of anger. "You keep calling me that and I'll show you that shootin' sample the hard way," he half-snarled.

Fargo reined the pinto to a halt, his eyes blue quartz. "You'll get your chance. That's a promise," he said quietly.

The younger man uttered a harsh snort and wheeled his horse away.

"What'd you do that for?" Athena asked, alarm in her voice. "You know he'll call you on it."

"But he'll wait. He's eager to shoot some Comanches first," Fargo said.

"And afterward?" she pressed.

Fargo's smile was thin. "I don't expect he'll have any afterward," he said. "Maybe none of us will," he added grimly, and spurred the pinto forward.

The terrain began to change into the long, flat slopes, the plateaus that would rise and take them into the desert mountains. The first plateau was strewn with rock and Fargo let the pinto pick his way with care. He glanced back to see the wagons bouncing up and down over the rocky terrain, shuddering and creaking, and his lips drew back in anger. He cantered back to Athena in the lead wagon.

"Slow down, goddammit," he barked.

She pulled on the reins and the team slacked its pace, the other wagons behind slowing at once. "Do you ever say anything nicely?" she asked, and there was real hurt in her voice.

"You ever use any common sense?" he snapped.

"I thought making time was important," she muttered.

Fargo leaned forward in the saddle. "You mean hurrying to prove your damn point, don't you?" he tossed at her. "You're so wrapped up in that, you can't think straight."

She said nothing, allowed herself to glower at him, and he whirled around, waved an arm forward.

They'd gone through the morning over the hard, rock-strewn ground when he heard the shout from behind, reined up to look back at the wagons. "Shit!" he muttered as he saw the reverend's Conestoga tilting hard, the rear wheel sticking out almost at right angles.

Others had clambered down from their wagons to gather around as he rode up, and he caught the apprehension on Judith Moreland's face as she watched him dismount. "One of the corner bolsters has snapped," Abe Sprain said on his hands and knees, peering under the wagon.

"We've two extras," the reverend said at once.

"You'll have to unload everything to fix it," Abe said as he got to his feet.

Fargo saw the reverend cast him a questioning glance. "Better get at it," Fargo said.

"I know you're thinking this is the result of overloading," the reverend began, and Fargo cut him off.

"No speeches, Reverend. Just get the damn wagon fixed," he growled.

Smith and Hawkins rode in and lent a hand along with the others as Fargo watched the pump organ slide down the little ramp first. He walked to one side, his eyes taking in the formation of pedestal rocks that rose up nearby. They stood in an almost churchlike series of vaulted forms, a kind of cathedral fashioned by wind and rain and burning sun, a desolate, silent beauty. He turned away, strolled down the line of wagons, his eyes cold as a frozen lake.

Darcy had boxes and trunks outside her wagon as he halted to peer at her. "Rearranging things better," she said. "Those damn rocks bounced everything around."

He saw a square, thinnish wooden box she had set to one side. "What's that?" he asked casually.

"My paintbox," she said as she went on shifting things in the wagon.

"Mind if I have a look?" he said as he flipped the latch open.

"Suit yourself," she said, intent on her chores. Fargo lifted the lid, his eyes moving across the neat row of tubes inside the box, a smooth palette wedged to one side. A half-dozen paintbrushes were neat in their own compartment.

"Very nice," he commented as he closed the lid.

Darcy leaned over to him, slid her arms around his neck. "Tonight?" she murmured, and he felt the soft pressure of her breasts against him.

"Definitely," he said, and pulled back out of the wagon.

Athena's eyes were spearing into him as he strolled away. "I see you've time to help some people and not others," she said coolly.

"The reverend's got all the help he needs," Fargo said mildly. "In fact, I'd say they're about finished." He strolled back to the Conestoga and Athena followed. The new corner bolster had been put in place and the wagon was being reloaded. The pump organ was the last piece left to go and he saw Judith come toward him, her round face full of apprehension again. She started to open her mouth, her eyes searching his face. "Get that organ on and let's move," he said. Judith's mouth snapped closed and her face lighted. She reached out impulsively, squeezed his arm, and spun around to the organ, where the reverend waited.

Fargo started back to the pinto as Athena watched him, her glance narrowed. He gave her a modest smile. "That's twice now you've been the milk of human kindness about that organ," Athena said. "Why don't I buy it?"

"I told you, honey, you've a suspicious nature. You'd better work on that," he said as he climbed onto the pinto, tossed her a smile, and rode off. The wagons began to roll forward again, more slowly this time, and by nightfall they'd reached the end of the first sloping plateau. He made camp on hard clay ground that was surrounded by pointed hillocks.

"Bring the sentries in closer tonight," he told Joe, taking the natural barriers into account. He rubbed down the pinto, ate with Joe, and had just washed off both tin plates when Herb Atkinson paused beside him.

"Things seem to be going well so far, don't they?" the man commented, and Fargo smiled at the unasked question.

"You talking about no Comanche?" he said.

Herb Atkinson half-shrugged. "I guess so," he murmured. "It's Mary. She's worried," he said. Fargo waited as he sought words. "That Quaker background of hers, it's still strong," the man said. "She remembers you asking if she could handle a rifle. She keeps thinking about it and she's not sure." Herb Atkinson looked uncomfortable. "Anything I can tell her?"

"Tell her to keep thinking about it," Fargo said grimly, and the man turned away, his face lengthened. Fargo started to walk from the camp area when Athena stepped out from between two of the wagons, her eyes narrowed at him.

"Why don't you ever sleep in camp?" she asked. "You've got sentries posted. Joe Pueblo is out there someplace. Seems to me you could bed down in camp."

He smiled at her. "You asking or inviting?"

Her eyes clouded at once. "Asking," she snapped.

"Too bad." He smiled as he moved on.

"Dammit, Fargo, don't you ever answer anything?" she called after him.

He let her question hang in silence as he picked up the bedroll and disappeared into the dark, her gasp of exasperation following after him as he made his way behind one of the pointed hillocks. He laid out his things, waited a few minutes, stepped from behind the hillock, walked halfway to the wagons until he saw Darcy moving uncertainly, peering at the line of hillocks. He moved toward her until she saw him. She wore the pink housedress and he took her hand, brought her behind the hillock where he'd put his things. Her arms started to slide around his neck at once, but he stepped back and drew a frown from her.

"After I get some answers," he said, and his voice was suddenly hard.

Her frown deepened. "Answers?" she echoed.

"That's right. I want to know what kind of game you're playing," he growled.

"Game? What are you talking about?" she returned, stared at him.

"You know damn well. Your little masquerade, it's over," he shot at her.

She pulled back, let herself look thoroughly confused. "I don't know what you're talking about," she said.

"I'm talking about you being a fake, a phony," Fargo snapped. "You're no more an artist than that rock over there."

He watched her let injured haughtiness take over her surprise, "What a ridiculous thing to say. Of course I'm an artist."

"Hell you are," he threw back. "I've known real artists, took one deep into the north country and the other across Boone's Trace. All they did was draw. Anything beautiful or different and they'd have their paints out or their sketch pad in hand. You've had a chance at things a real artist would jump at painting, including the red-tail cactus in flower. You were busy cleaning trail dust off your boots when a real artist would've been painting his damn head off."

"I just haven't got started yet," she tried.

"Bull," he barked.

"You saw my paintbox," she countered.

He gave a harsh laugh. "Yes, I saw it. Not a brush that was used, every tube of paint brand-new," he said.

"It's a new paintbox," she answered.

"It's for show only. You put it together, but you forgot a few things: turpentine, rags, and a palette knife for scraping off paint. Hell, there's no real artist has a paintbox without turpentine, rags, and a palette knife."

"I have them someplace else," she tried, but now she was sounding only lame.

Fargo's hand shot out, closed around the front of the pink housedress, and yanked her forward, and her short hair bounced up and down.

"The truth, dammit, no more games," he roared. "Start talking or I'll tell Athena I think you're a ringer sent by Ellsworth Pond. It'll be a long, lonely trail back for you."

"I'm no such thing," Darcy protested hotly.

"Then what the hell are you?" he demanded, and watched the bitter anger swim into her eyes as she glowered back.

"Let go of me first," she muttered.

Damn, she was a dogged little package, he swore inwardly as he released his hold on her. She stepped back, smoothed the front of the housedress, her lips pressed tight on each other. She raised her eyes to meet Fargo's waiting stare.

"My name's Darcy Dennison," she said.

Fargo felt the frown slide across his brow as thoughts clicked in his mind and he let them find voice. "Dennison . . . Maynard Dennison . . . Colonel Maynard Dennison," he murmured.

"My father," she said, and he heard the quiet pride in her voice.

Answers began to take shape inside him at once, but he held back, wanting her words for them. "Go on," he growled.

"I heard about Athena Neils, how she was saying all kinds of things, trying to lay the blame on somebody for what happened," Darcy said. "I wasn't going to stand by and let her blacken my father's name and reputation. When I heard about the wagon train she was putting together, I decided to join up."

"So you got yourself a wagon, a new name, and a story to go with it," Fargo said.

"That's right," Darcy said defiantly. "I wanted to be right here on the spot so she couldn't get away with a lot of loose talk and things twisted to fit what she wants to see."

"What if Athena's right?" Fargo asked. "What if there is blame and maybe a lot more?"

"Then it didn't have anything to do with my father," Darcy threw back hotly.

"He was part of some things I can't understand, things that can't be explained away just like that," Fargo said, his voice hard.

"Dammit, he was killed, too," Darcy flung out, and there was a sob in her voice.

"That's why I'm here, because nothing makes any damn sense in this whole business," Fargo said.

"Maybe it never will," Darcy returned. "All Athena Neils wants is to find a scapegoat."

"You ever think maybe she wants to find the truth?" Fargo speared back.

"That's all I care about," Darcy said. "The truth and my father's name."

"Is it?" Fargo frowned. "You've been using your little beaver to try and buy me. You figured if I was wrapped up enough in you I wouldn't be partial to Athena's side when the time came." He watched Darcy's lips tighten as he went on. "Only you were wasting your time. I can be balled but not bought, honey. Now you get your tricky little tail the hell out of my sight."

She didn't move, her Cupid's-bow mouth set into a kind of pout. "No," she said almost too softly to hear.

"What?" Fargo frowned. "Damn, you stubborn or stupid?"

"Neither," she said, shaking her head. "It's all out now, in the open. No more games. I want to stay for the right reasons this time."

He peered hard at her. "You won't be buying one damn thing," he warned.

"I know," she said, her arms sliding around his neck. "And I want to stay." Her mouth came to his, pressing, asking, wanting, and he felt her opening the pink housedress for him. She sank down onto the bedroll, slipping naked out of the housedress, hands pulling at his clothes. She lifted her pelvis, offering all she had offered before but with no guile now, no trying to buy his spirit. She meant it, he was certain. She believed herself, as if hope could be tossed aside like a used shoe. He slid through the warm gateway and she cried out and there was no time left for thinking or feeling sorry for her.

She made love with a new urgency, straining to extract the last gasp of ecstasy from every moment, and finally she lay beside him in exhaustion, slender body slowly unwinding. He held her until she moved to sit up and draw the pink garment around herself, her face quiet with inner thoughts. "You'll be telling Athena, I suppose," she slid out.

"It has to be said," he answered. "I thought maybe you'd rather do it."

She considered a moment, nodded slowly. "Give me a little time," she asked.

"Don't take too long," he said, and she rose, her face grave, a sadness drawn around her like a cloak. She slowly walked from him and he watched till she disappeared around the side of the hillock. Fargo lay back and felt the sourness inside him. There would only be pain out of it. One was committed to defend, the other to accuse. One was certain of innocence, the other of guilt. Darcy could see her father only as an honorable man, as blameless for what had happened as any of the other victims. Athena saw him as part of a massacre that had somehow been arranged, a victim of his own complicity.

Someone would know the face of pain and bitterness.

5

It was an unsmiling morning, he saw as he sipped from the tin cup of strong coffee. All except Judith, whose round face wore bright cheerfulness. Darcy's eyes were darkened, her face tight, as she met his glance in a silent exchange. Athena had saved a resentful glare from the night before for him as she hitched up her wagon with Abe Sprain's help. Herb and Mary Atkinson seemed wrapped in their own silence and Fargo let his gaze linger on Henrietta Crown, saw the burning eyes scanning the land ahead with an intensity that was almost frightening. Fargo drained the coffee, made a face at the last sharpness of it, and nodded to Joe as he started to ride out.

The morning sun rose quickly as the wagons broke camp and Fargo took in the terrain with a grunt of satisfaction, flat, hard land made for making good time with few of the axle-breaking stones that had littered the last day's ride. He allowed only a few rest stops and by late afternoon they had almost reached the end of the second long, gradually sloping plateau. Fargo peered through the shimmering heat waves that drifted into the air. The high land of Condor Pass remained beyond sight, but the land grew more uneven, rock formations and gulleys dotting the horizon.

He continued on, spurred the pinto forward, and had

moved a few hundred yards ahead of the wagons when he saw Joe Pueblo waiting, the gelding halted beside a line of mesquite. Fargo reined up beside him and his eyes narrowed as they moved back and forth across the horizon. He halted as he peered to the left, almost across from where they stood, peered deep into the horizon line. Joe Pueblo grunted and Fargo nodded his reply, his eyes focused in the distance, which was starting to turn blue-gray with the coming dusk.

Athena was the first to roll up, Darcy's wagon edging halfway alongside, and Fargo saw Athena's frown seek him out. "Something wrong?" she questioned.

"Just some riders moving along out there," Fargo said, nodding with his head toward the southern horizon line.

Athena's eyes followed. "That dust cloud out there?" she asked.

"That's right," Fargo told her.

"Comanche?" Athena asked, the eagerness again coming into her voice.

"Hah!" Joe Pueblo spit out.

"What's that mean?" Athena snapped.

"It means any Comanches raising that much dust would be drummed out of the tribe," Fargo translated.

"Then what is it?" Athena asked.

Fargo's eyes stayed narrowed as he peered into the distance. "Maybe a posse. Maybe some folks running from a posse. Maybe a herd of mustangs. Make your own guess," he said. "Keep moving on. It'll be dark soon."

He spurred the pinto into a trot, rode ahead, and was waiting when the wagons rolled to a halt. He'd chosen a spot that dipped to form a shallow hollow in the flatland, and he held back till everyone was settled in before he made his way to Athena's wagon and rapped on the tailgate. She came out, her hair down and a thin robe hastily thrown around her shoulders. In the dim light of a flickering candle from inside the wagon she looked softly lovely, the smooth round curve of her breasts lifting from the top of the robe. But the hardness in his eyes stayed. "I want to talk," he growled.

"Something in your craw?" she asked.

"I want you to stop being so damned eager to see Comanche signs," he said.

"Why? Does that bother you?" she asked, her eyebrows lifting.

"I don't like it. It's as if you're just begging for trouble," he growled.

Her seawater eyes took on a cool blue green. "Superstitious? You afraid I'm calling the evil spirits down on us? You do surprise me," she said with sweet acid.

"Then just chalk it up to my one-quarter Cherokee blood," Fargo tossed back. "But I'll be damned glad if we never see any Comanche signs."

Athena's eyes turned dark blue. "Finding signs is important. You know why. I thought you agreed what it would mean. I thought you cared about learning the truth," she said.

"I do, but not if it means wishing the Comanche on our heads. Now, you just lay back some, dammit," he said angrily, turned, and strode away and felt the defensiveness simmering in her. He heard the slap of the canvas as she went back inside the wagon and he walked to the pinto and began to carry his bedroll toward the rise of the hollow. He halted as he saw Darcy standing beside her wagon in the pink housedress. She took the few steps to his side. "No place fit for a visit tonight," he said.

"I know," she said. "Maybe it's best."

"Maybe," he said. "There'll be other nights for you to decide that."

She nodded and returned to her wagon and he waited till she'd slipped inside before going on. He'd just settled down when Joe Pueblo appeared, the gelding behind him.

"I'm riding out," he said, and Fargo questioned with his eyes. "My skin itches," Joe said. "There is Navaho campground a half-day from here. Maybe I find out something there."

"You know where we'll be heading," Fargo said. "You can pick us up easy enough."

Joe Pueblo grunted agreement and climbed onto the gelding. He walked the horse quietly into the night and Fargo let his eyes sweep the edges of the little hollow. Smith and Broadman had drawn first sentry shifts and he picked out their shapes in the night. He let his eyes slowly circle the edge of the little hollow again, move along the line of the wagons. They came to a halt, narrowed. Henrietta Crown stood at the rear wheel of her wagon, barely visible, blond-gray hair a silvery blur in the night. She stood motionless, staring out into the darkness beyond the edge of the hollow.

Fargo lay down on his bedroll, the woman's haunted image staying with him. This was a caravan of questions, outer and inner ones, and he wondered if perhaps Henrietta Crown would be the one without an answer. He turned on his side and slept as the night stayed still.

The morning came in with a shimmering heat that rose in waves from the dry ground. Fargo moved the wagons slowly, took a number of stops and used the extra horses to spell at least one half of each team. They had halted a little past the noon hour and he wandered over to where Darcy was adjusting a harness buckle. "This is as good a time as any," he murmured quietly.

Her eyes held solemnness. "No, not now. I can't just go to her and make it an announcement, my name's not Darcy Clark," she protested. "I'll find the right time and the right place, believe me, Fargo," she said.

"I won't wait much longer," he warned her as he turned away, his glance moving across the wagons. Only Judith seemed unaffected by the heat; she hummed a hymn while she adjusted the canvas at the rear of the

Conestoga. Bud Denny lounged against Athena's wagon, idly twirling his Walker Colt, snapping it up sharply every third or fourth time in mock firing position. His mouth took on its confidently arrogant twist as he saw Fargo watching his little display.

Athena stepped from the wagon, her hair pulled atop her head and her neck looking beautifully long and graceful. Fargo saw Bud Denny's cold eyes follow her the way a diamondback follows a prairie chicken. He turned and lifted himself onto the pinto as he wondered if he could keep Bud Denny in line long enough. He motioned the wagons forward and the caravan slowly set off again.

The land grew steeper, no less dry but with the topsoil less marked by water-starved cracks. They'd gone a few hours into the afternoon when the lone horseman came into view, moving toward them from the west. As the rider drew near, Fargo brought the wagons to a halt, moved a few feet forward of the lead wagon as the horseman stopped. The man stayed in the saddle, a tall, rangy figure wearing a tan Stetson, a tan fringed buckskin vest, and a layer of trail dust. The man's eyes scanned the wagons, came to rest on the big black-haired figure on the Ovaro. "You Fargo?" he asked out of a long-jawed face.

Fargo nodded. "And you?"

"Jack Taylor," the man answered as he pushed his Stetson back with one thumb. "You got an Indian friend name of Joe Pueblo?" he asked.

"I do," Fargo said.

"Well, he's been hurt some," the man said.

"Hurt?" Fargo frowned.

"Broken leg, I'd say," the man replied. "Two friends of mine and me, we came on him laying on the ground, damn near dried up from the sun. He told us his horse bolted at a rattler and threw him."

Fargo frowned in concern. "Damn," he muttered.

"He sent me to tell you to come get him," the man said.

"He did, eh?" Fargo grunted, and let the frown of concern stay on his face.

"Yep," the man answered.

"Well, I guess I've got to go back with you. I owe Joe a few," Fargo said. "What'd you say your name was?"

"Taylor, Jack Taylor," the man said.

"All right, I'll be right along, Jack," Fargo said, and the man nodded, moved his horse a dozen yards away as Fargo turned to Athena. "You just go on and make camp as usual, come dark," he instructed. "I'd guess it'll be plenty late before I can get back with Joe."

He saw the mixed emotions swim in her eyes. "I know you have to go," she said. "But what if you don't get back? What if something unexpected happens?"

He let a little smile tease at her. "I'd be touched if I thought you were worrying just about me," he said.

She met his eyes with a half-glower. "You're included," she returned.

He took the teasing out of his smile. "Then I'll be sure to be back. You can count on it," he said. He swept the others with a quick glance as they watched, concern on every face, and he gave a quick wave of his hand as he swung the pinto around and rode to where the man waited.

"All set," he said as the man started to move on. "Where's Joe now?"

"About an hour's ride from here," the man said. "We moved him out of the sun into a gulley with some rock shade."

"Much obliged to you," Fargo said warmly.

"Folks got to help each other out here," Jack Taylor said.

"No arguing with that," Fargo agreed emphatically. "What are you doing out this way, Jack?"

"We were down Mexico way with some mustangs. Just started heading back to Colorado," the man answered.

"Joe have anything else to say?" Fargo asked casually.

"No, except that he hoped I'd find you and bring you back quick," the man answered.

"You did just that." Fargo smiled as he sat back in the saddle, rode easily, and lapsed into silence except to whistle a little tune now and then. His eyes moved back and forth across the distant horizon as they rode, almost idly, and they'd ridden almost an hour when he let the pinto fall back a half-length behind the other horse. He went on another half-mile, then reined up sharply. The other man turned at once, pulled his horse up.

"Somethin' wrong?" He frowned.

"You could say that." Fargo smiled amiably as he saw the man stare at the big Colt in his hand, a frown quickly wiping away the initial surprise on his face.

"What the hell's all this about?" the man growled.

"It's about telling lies. It can get you in trouble," Fargo said.

"What lies, mister?" the man protested.

"About doing good deeds," Fargo said chidingly.

"I didn't lie. Your Indian pal's waitin' in the ravine right now," the man insisted.

"I'll buy that much. Only you didn't find him. You bushwhacked him, somehow," Fargo said.

"You got somethin' figured all wrong, mister," the man protested again.

Fargo's smile was thin. "You had Joe Pueblo figured all wrong," he said.

The man's eyes narrowed. "What the hell does that mean?" he rasped.

"First, no horse would've thrown Joe Pueblo. Maybe, just maybe, in the timberland but not out here in this country," Fargo said. "Second, Joe Pueblo would never ask me to leave the wagon train. He'd never have sent you to bring me to him. It was a good story, only it didn't fit the man."

The other man's eyes narrowed as he stared back. "Get off that horse, slow and easy," Fargo ordered. He saw the man hesitate, eye the Colt. "One wrong move and you'll buy a bullet in your gut," Fargo said. The man pushed his thoughts aside and swung one leg down from the horse, then the other. "Now drop your gun belt," Fargo ordered. He moved the Colt a fraction, aimed it at the man's midsection as the man unbuckled the gun belt and let it fall to the ground. Fargo slid from the pinto, the Colt unwavering. With one foot, he kicked the gun belt to the side. "Now take off the hat and that buckskin jacket," he ordered.

"Why?" the man questioned truculently.

"Off. My temper's wearing thin," Fargo said, and an edge colored his tone. The man obeyed sullenly, dropped his jacket and hat in a pile. "On the ground, facedown," Fargo ordered. The man eyed the Colt again and decided to drop to his knees and lower himself to his stomach. Fargo slipped off his own shirt and his wide-brimmed hat and tossed them beside the prostrate figure. "Get up and put them on," he said as he stepped back and scooped up the fringed buckskin jacket and the tan Stetson.

As the man started to get up, Fargo slipped on the jacket and the tan Stetson. The man glowered at him as he put on the shirt and the wide-brimmed hat. Fargo took his lariat from the saddle and approached the man. "Your arms out front," he ordered, his eyes watching the man's face. He caught the flicker that passed through the long-jawed face, braced himself as the man sprang forward, one hand reaching to knock the Colt aside. Fargo half-spun away, pulled his finger from the trigger, and brought the Colt forward in a sharp, ramrod thrust. The gun sank into the man's abdomen and Fargo felt the figure go limp instantly.

"Agh. . . . Jesus," the man gasped as he pitched forward to his knees, clutching one hand to his stomach. Fargo brought the butt of the Colt down on the back of his neck and the man half-rolled, half-sank to the ground.

Fargo pushed him aside with his foot and took the lariat from his saddle, turned the unconscious form over, and tied the man's hands in front of him. He left a length of rope dangling from the wrist bonds and stepped back as the man groaned, blinked his eyes open, groaned again, and slowly managed to focus his vision.

"On your feet," Fargo said, and waited as Jack Taylor slowly pushed himself upright on his wrist-bound hands. Fargo jammed his own wide-brimmed hat onto the man's head.

"This won't be foolin' anybody," the man rasped.

"Did I say anything about fooling anyone?" Fargo asked mildly. "Now we switch horses. Get on my pinto," he ordered, and almost smiled as he saw the moment of surprised fright flash in the man's eyes. "Something wrong?" he inquired. "Somebody expecting I'll be on an Ovaro?"

"Nobody's expectin' nothin'," the man growled, recovering enough to let hate push aside the flash of fear.

"That's good," Fargo said. "Now get your ass on that horse." He raised the Colt and the man grasped the saddle horn with both hands to pull himself onto the pinto. Fargo wrapped the remaining length of lariat around the saddle horn and strapped the man's hands tightly in place. He stepped back, surveyed the figure in satisfaction. The switch was more than good enough for anything but close-range inspection, and there'd be none of that. He swung himself up on Jack Taylor's horse and rode beside the pinto, moving forward unhurriedly until the outline of rock appeared in the distance. He shot a glance at Jack Taylor. The man peered ahead, his face sullen and drawn tight.

Fargo increased their pace and the rock formation took shape, the gulley opening downward with a line of rocks on each side. He cast another glance at Jack Taylor. Uneasiness strained his face, but he rode grim-lipped, still clinging to some hope that he'd find a way out, surly defiance in his eyes. Fargo felt his own cold anger growing colder. He rummaged into the pockets of the buckskin jacket and found a kerchief and grunted in satisfaction. It made it unnecessary to waste his own. He leaned over in the saddle, moved with swift roughness, grasping the man's jaw with one hand and forcing his mouth open. He pushed the kerchief into the man's mouth with the other hand, pressed it deep, continued to push and press until he had the entire kerchief stuffed into the man's mouth as Jack Taylor tried to gasp and protest. He let go of the man's jaw when the last of the kerchief was pushed into place. It would stay there long enough.

"Breathe through your nose," he said coldly. "You don't have much breathing time left anyway."

He saw fury mixed with fear in the man's eyes and heard the harsh wheezing sound of his breath as it was forced through his nostrils. He rode out in front of the Ovaro and the horse followed his lead. He stayed in single file as he led the way to the mouth of the gulley, glanced back at Jack Taylor. The final proof lay in the man's face, desperation bulging his eyes, lines of perspiration running down his face under the wide-brimmed hat. The man had been sent as a Judas sheep to lead him to his death, and Fargo turned away, able to feel nothing but a sense of icy justice. His hand moved to rest lightly on the butt of the Colt at his side.

He rode deeper into the gulley with the tan Stetson pulled low and his eyes flicking from one side of the rocks to the other. Behind him, the man was trying to cry out but he managed only a barely audible, strangulated wheeze. Fargo didn't glance back, his eyes searching the sides of the gulley. He didn't see Joe Pueblo but he didn't expect they'd have him in plain sight. He'd reached the bottom of the gulley where it began to level off when he saw the figures appear on the rocks to his right. The first two that stepped into view carried Spencer carbines; the second two, handguns.

As he rode on, he saw the two figures raise their rifles and the gulley reverberated to the heavy sound of the rifle fire, a volley of shots. Fargo heard the bullets slam into the figure behind him, a heavy, thudding sound. The Colt leaped into his hand as he twisted in the saddle and fired, targeting the riflemen first. He saw the nearest one stagger backward as if pulled by an invisible string, to suddenly disappear below the rocks. The second one seemed to toss his rifle exuberantly into the air as he twisted and dived headfirst from the top of the rocks. As the other two still stared in astonishment, Fargo vaulted from the saddle. He was on the ground, diving behind a line of low rocks by the time they recovered. He fired a shot that narrowly missed one of the figures diving for cover, saw the other man leap out of sight. His glance went to the Ovaro, to see the man's figure hanging lifelessly from the horse, feet dragging on the ground, his wrists still bound to the saddle horn. An oozing flow of red seeped out of his kerchief-filled mouth. Fargo gave a low whistle and the pinto came forward. The horse shielding him from the opposite rocks, he stepped forward, took out his Arkansas throwing knife, and severed the rope holding the man's wrists to the saddle horn. He jumped back behind his rock cover as the pinto trotted away and the bullet-ridden body dropped to the ground.

His eyes scanned the rocks across from him. He saw nothing, but his ears picked up the scrape of footsteps, half-sliding, half-scurrying. They were going to talk things over, and Fargo's eyes went to the sky to see the gray-purple dusk moving over the gulley. He moved back from the edge of the rocks, spied a passageway, and staying low, moved up it to a higher spot. Another passage beckoned, and with the silence of a panther on the prowl, he moved upward again, halted behind a pair of rounded stones that afforded a good view of the gulley below and the surrounding rocks. He settled down to wait. motionless as a lizard on a rock, concentrating all his senses on listening.

He glanced upward again and saw the night moving in quickly and he guessed there were perhaps another fifteen minutes of daylight left. He half-smiled as he picked up the sounds from the edge of the line of rocks at his side. One had circled around to make his way along his side of the rocks, hurrying while there was still light. Fargo inclined his head, strained his ears to pick up what he knew he'd hear. He smiled again as the sound reached him, the other man coming in from the back where he'd crossed over. He lifted his head to peer across the gulley, his eyes moving down to the end of the rocks where he saw the opening, the only one large enough for their horses. That explained why they were coming after him in such a hurry. He had too good coverage of the only way out of the gulley. He pulled his head back down and slid himself half under a flat rock. It allowed him only a narrow field of vision but gave them no chance at a clear shot at him.

He continued to wait and heard them coming in close, moving more carefully now, but their movements easy to follow. They were making short, fast moves, halting after each one to peer down into the cracks and crevices, ready to blaze away, of course. His eyes stayed fixed on the narrow space above where he lay half-hidden. The light was growing dim when he heard their scraping steps almost directly above. He moved his arm forward, raising the Colt upward, his finger resting on the trigger. The two figures came into view above him, but they needed a moment to peer down into the dimness, find their quarry. Fargo's Colt barked first and the one man screamed and clutched at his groin. The scream became a guttural sound as he pitched forward, both hands still pressed to his belly as though they could hold back the gusher of red that erupted. Fargo glimpsed the other figure leaping out of sight, heard the man scrambling furiously away, and his eyes went to the man lying like a broken figurine a few feet from him, his neck twisted grotesquely where he'd landed against the rocks, his hands still clutched to his belly, a rigid death grip now.

Fargo pushed himself from under the slab, paused to hear the sounds of the other man still scrambling across the rocks. He was running to return to the other side of the gulley, Fargo realized, as the darkness descended. Fargo climbed unhurriedly down from the place, made his way along the bottom of the rocks until he was opposite the wide passageway on the other side. He could see two of the horses back in the rocks and he settled down to wait, his eyes fixed on the passageway. Not more than fifteen minutes had gone by when he picked out the movement in the deep shadows of the passageway and he heard the sound of a horse being carefully edged along the side of the rocks. He fired a shot, heard it ping off the stones, and the sound of horse and man scurrying backward followed instantly.

Fargo settled back again, reloaded the Colt. He had only five minutes to wait this time when the voice called out, the sound traveling clearly in the little gulley. "Fargo, you listenin'?" the man called. Fargo stayed silent and he could almost hear the man cursing to himself. "Fargo," the man called again. "I got your Indian friend here." Again Fargo remained silent. "You hear me, dammit?" the man cursed.

"I hear you," Fargo said. "I want to hear him."

A moment of silence followed, time to remove a gag.

Then he heard Joe Pueblo's voice. "I'm okay, Fargo," he said.

"Okay, Joe," Fargo returned.

The man's voice cut in. "His life for mine, Fargo," he offered.

The Trailsman's lips pursed and he scanned the opposite line of rocks, his thoughts racing. He could try to stall and make his way close enough to the man without being heard. But he couldn't count on the man. Perhaps his nerves were close to the breaking point. He might suddenly grow alarmed and make good on his threat. It was too risky. Fargo lifted his voice.

"No tricks or you're a dead man," he said.

"No tricks," the man answered. "I'm coming down."

"Come on," Fargo said, rising to his feet but staying in the shadows beside the rock. He heard the movement in the passageway and moments later Joe Pueblo appeared, hands tied behind his back. The man was close behind him, a gun pressed into the small of his back, leading the horse with his other hand. He used Joe as a shield as well. Fargo, the Colt in his hand, stepped forward, his eyes narrowed as the man continued to walk forward, staying close to the rocks as he moved up the gulley. Fargo watched him glance nervously back at his figure waiting with the Colt poised. The man had gone halfway up the gulley when Fargo called out.

"That's far enough," he said. "Hit the saddle."

He saw the man hesitate, unsure whether to hold to his bargain, and Fargo pulled the trigger back on the Colt. The soft click echoed loudly in the silence of the gulley. The man turned, pushed Joe Pueblo out of the way, and vaulted onto the horse, lying flat in the saddle as he sent the animal galloping up the gulley. Fargo felt his finger tremble on the trigger but he held back. A bargain was a bargain, even made with a hyena. The galloping horse disappeared into the darkness and Fargo strode to where Joe waited, cut the wrist ropes, and Joe rubbed circulation back into his arms.

"I owe you one, Fargo," he said.

"How'd they nail you?" Fargo asked.

"On way back from Navaho camp. Old trick. I went for it," Joe said, and looked pained. "I see man on ground near rocks, no horse, looks dead maybe. I go see if I can help."

"And the rest of them popped up," Fargo finished. Joe nodded, spat on the ground in disgust. "Not your fault," Fargo said. "It's old, but it'll keep working so long as people try to help each other." He lifted his arms and pulled off the buckskin jacket and tossed the Stetson on the ground with it. As Joe went up into the rocks to retrieve his horse, Fargo whistled softly and the Ovaro came from the far end of the gulley to halt beside him. He dug a shirt from his saddlebag, stepped to the lifeless figure of Jack Taylor, and took his own wide-brimmed hat back. He was in the saddle and ready to ride when Joe returned.

"We have one answer," Joe Pueblo said as they rode from the gulley. "Ellsworth Pond very afraid not very hurt."

"He sent those bushwhackers?" Fargo asked. "I was thinking that way."

"They talk about his orders when they wait for you to come back," Joe said.

Fargo grunted. "So we know that much now. You hear anything from the Navaho?"

"Comanche damn mad about something, they say. Condor Pass make Molokah number-one chief now."

Fargo's lips set grimly and he turned thoughts in his mind as he quickened the pace through the night. Pond had something to be afraid of, that much was clear now. He'd obviously been behind the attempt to set the wagons on fire. But that was the only thing clear. What and why and all the other strange things were still unexplained. Fargo was still tossing thoughts in his head when they reached the place where the wagons camped in a small circle. Amos Alder and Abe Sprain were standing sentry duty, relief flooding their faces when they recognized the riders. There were a few hours left till dawn and Fargo bedded down at once, slept hard until he woke early. He was sipping fresh coffee when Athena emerged from her tent and saw him.

"You're back," she squealed in joy, rushed forward, started to throw her arms around him, and then pulled back.

"Don't stop," he protested as she recovered her usual control.

"I am glad you're back," she said, and he saw the others hurrying from their wagons to gather around. Darcy in her turned-up blouse looked at him with round, questioning eyes. Her head turned with everyone else's as Joe Pueblo came forward to pour himself a cup of coffee.

"His leg healed up fast," Fargo said dryly.

Athena stared back with her eyes wide, a frown slipping across her smooth brow. "It was a lie . . . all of it, a trick," she breathed.

"Give the lady a cigar," Fargo said, finishing his coffee.

"They wanted you," Athena went on, thinking aloud. "Ellsworth Pond. Getting rid of you would be turning us back."

"Or maybe ensuring another massacre," Fargo ventured.

Athena didn't hide the triumph in her face and this time she hugged him impulsively. "I was right," she said. "I was right all along."

"There's still too much that doesn't add up," Fargo said.

"It will," she said, pulling back. "It'll all add up. Condor Pass was planned, just as I said, and now Pond is afraid I'll be able to prove all of it, his part and Colonel Dennison's part."

Fargo's eyes found Darcy, saw her face had turned chalk-white.

"No," Darcy blurted out. "Colonel Dennison didn't do anything wrong."

Athena turned in surprise and Darcy stepped forward to face her. Fargo saw her hands were clenched so tight the knuckles were dead white. "My name's not Darcy Clark. It's Darcy Dennison," she bit out.

The surprise deepened in Athena's face for a moment, slid into a thin, haughty half-smile. "Darcy Dennison," she repeated slowly. "Now, isn't that revealing? Colonel Maynard Dennison's daughter, I presume."

"Exactly," Darcy snapped.

Athena stayed coolly calm, Fargo saw. "Here to defend Daddy, are you?" she speared.

"Here to see that you don't ruin a man's reputation with a lot of wild, unfounded charges," Darcy flung back angrily.

"So you lied your way into my wagon train. Deceit seems to run in the family," Athena said.

Darcy's hand shot out, smashed against Athena's cheek. "*Bitch!*" she hissed.

Fargo saw Athena take a half-step back, her cheek reddening instantly. Darcy, quivering with rage, held her hands stiffly at her sides. She didn't expect the return slap that sent her head twisting to one side as Athena struck with surprising force. "Liar," she flung back.

Fargo saw Darcy fight back tears, anger, frustration, uncertainty pulling at her while Athena was bolstered by the feeling of triumph and the power of her convictions. "My father was hired to do a job," she said. "That doesn't make him part of anything else."

"He was part of it," Athena said with icy conviction.

"You can't go around maligning my father," Darcy shouted at her.

"I can do anything I please. My father was killed in that massacre," Athena exploded in fury.

"So was mine," Darcy threw back. "Doesn't that mean anything to you?"

Fargo cut in harshly. "That's one of the pieces that don't add up," he said.

Athena turned a chiding glance at him. "It will," she said. "You really can't think there's any doubt now, can you?" she said.

"I never call a hand till I see the last card," he said. "Now, I think everybody best get ready to move. We're getting a late start as it is," he said.

The others slowly turned away with a hush of murmured confidences and Fargo saw Athena's glance following Darcy "She lied her way into this wagon train I don't see any reason why she should stay on," Athena muttered crossly.

"She stays. She's got a stake in the truth, whatever it is," Fargo said.

Athena's eyes were coolly curious. "You keep surprising me. Such understanding and sympathy," she commented.

"Sympathy, hell," the voice intruded with a harsh laugh, and Fargo saw Bud Denny nearby. "He just doesn't want her to stop bringing it to him," the man said with malicious glee.

Fargo watched Athena's mouth open, the seawater eyes turn a cold blue. "Go on," she said to Bud Denny, her voice almost hushed.

"I sleep light. I've seen her sneaking back lots of nights," Bud Denny said. He threw back his head to laugh again as he strode away, and Fargo met Athena's blue-flame eyes.

"You've been on her side all along," she accused.

"On her side, on top of her, and underneath her, too, but not the way you mean," he said.

"And none of that affected you, of course," she said with heavy sarcasm.

"Not from the waist up," he answered.

"You expect me to believe that?" she asked.

"You damnwell better," he growled. "I agreed to help you get this wagon train through and find out the truth about Condor Pass. I've done some on that already. You keep being so cussed and I'll come get a down payment on the rest of our deal."

Her eyes widened. "You wouldn't," she gasped.

"Hell, I wouldn't," he said.

"Dammit, Fargo, I don't know what you're made of," Athena said.

"The best and the worst," he told her. "Now pull these wagons out." He strode to the pinto and swung into the saddle, saw Bud Denny and trotted over to him. The thin smile twisted the younger man's lips at once. "A loose tongue can get you in trouble," Fargo remarked calmly.

"You calling me? You ready to see about fast shootin'." Bud Denny asked at once.

"Not yet," Fargo said.

The younger man's mouth took on arrogance. "Time's going to run out on you one of these days," he said, and laughed with cold anticipation.

"Guess so." Fargo nodded as he moved away. The wagons were pulling out, Athena in the lead. Darcy was swinging into third place, sitting very straight, but in her quick glance he saw the pain behind the defensiveness. He rode out beside Joe Pueblo and watched the land rise more sharply even as it remained dry and hot.

Midday brought an unexpected gift as they came

upon a rise of chalkstone with a pair of clear water sinkholes in the midst of the formation. A line of low stones and a growth of cholla bushes formed a loose curtain in front of the two pools.

"Ladies first," Fargo said as he dismounted, relaxed on the ground, and listened to the sounds coming from the sinkholes. Darcy returned first, her short hair dry, her skin scrubbed and shiny, but her eyes still troubled. The men followed when the women finished, and Fargo waited till last, finally climbed to the twin pools, and tossed clothes off to sink into water that was more warm than cool. It still felt thoroughly refreshing and he washed, pulled himself from the pool to stand naked for a moment. As he sank down to stretch out in the sun, he knew he wasn't alone. Someone was watching from behind the cholla. He felt it, sensed it, with that wild-creature part of him. He stretched his beautifully proportioned, hard-muscled body out flat. Not Darcy, he was sure. She'd no reason to play Peeping Tom. Athena's face swam before his half-closed eyes and he smiled inwardly. She'd not be above a little surreptitious ogling. Or perhaps closed-in, pent-up Mary Atkinson. Or—and the furrow pressed into his forehead—perhaps no one from the wagons. His hand slid almost motionlessly to the Colt in the holster on the ground at his side, closed around the gun. He remained still, eyes half-closed, but every muscle had grown taut and then he heard the soft scrape of footsteps hurrying away. He sat up, pulled on clothes, and stepped through the cholla, scanned the ground. The hard rock told him nothing and he returned to the wagons.

They rolled onward minutes later and Fargo pulled up beside Darcy, peered at the tightness in her face. "Fighting inside yourself won't help any," he offered. "Time will do the telling."

She flung a glance made of pride and defensiveness.

"My father wasn't part of a plan to massacre twenty people and himself. That's what time will tell," she snapped.

"Could well be," Fargo soothed agreeably, and moved on. As he drew alongside Athena's lead wagon, he saw her spear him with a glance of acid sweetness.

"A little tender comforting?" she tossed out.

"You hear?" he asked.

"No, but I didn't need to," she said. "You can give her nice words. I'll take the hard facts."

"Maybe you'd best remember something," he said. "Facts and truth aren't always the same thing." He rode on, not waiting for an answer.

Joe Pueblo was riding point and Fargo caught up to him, let his eyes travel across the horizon, move along the sloping where it began to rise more sharply and became studded with rainwash-sculpted mountain rock. In the dim distance he could see the harsh desert mountains rising suddenly, no green foothills to act as a bed. Condor Pass was in those mountains of granite buttresses and etched sandstone, another day's ride, he estimated. A line of tall saguaro cactus came into view, resembling a troop of soldiers standing at attention. Fargo steered the pinto along the line of the tall cactus, his eyes narrowed as he peered at the thick base of each one. He halted, gestured with a nod, and Joe Pueblo grunted.

Fargo halted before the next in line, did the same with the one that stood beside it, and again Joe Pueblo nodded. The wagons rolled up, Athena first, Darcy swinging out of line to come up closer.

"What is it?" Athena questioned.

"Comanche," Fargo said.

Athena's eyes swept the ground, gazed in alarm across the distant land. "Where?" she asked.

"They were here," Fargo said. He pointed to the base

of the towering saguaro, where a deep cut into the plant had been made, a V-shaped slice that had been neatly put back in place. "They took water from the saguaro," Fargo said. "Each one of these can hold a ton or more of water stored inside it. The Comanche know how to use these cactus growths and that cut is their mark."

"How long ago?" he heard Abe Sprain's voice question.

Fargo bent down to the cut in the cactus. "Maybe six hours ago," he said.

Darcy's voice cut in. "How can you be so sure? There's not a mark on the ground, not a single hoofprint," she protested.

"Comanche made of tricks," Joe Pueblo grunted.

"Marks on this hard ground are all surface prints, made of trail dust. The last rider drags a blanket held out by two poles. It wipes away any tracks," Fargo explained.

"But you knew what to look for," Athena said. "Marks, signs, the Comanche tricks, you picked them up. Others should have, isn't that so, Fargo?" she added, unable to keep a waspish triumph out of her voice. "Someone experienced in Comanche ways?"

"Possibly," he answered.

Athena's eyes flashed. "Dammit, you're hedging," she shot back.

"No hedging," he said. "Why'd you come to me?"

"Because you're the very best, the Trailsman," she said.

"That's right. I see things others miss, even experienced men. It comes from inside somewhere, an instinct, a feel, call it whatever you like," he said.

Athena's lips pulled in grudging concession and she half-shrugged. "Now what?" she said.

"Keep moving. I want to make camp at the base of those mountains ahead," he said.

Abe Sprain's voice cut in with a grimness that echoed

the faces of the others as they looked on. "Then the Comanche are here, someplace near enough," he said.

"They're here and they know we're here," Fargo said. He didn't need to add anything more. It was in Abe Sprain's face, and the grim faces of the others, as they began to move the wagons forward. Fargo rode ahead, Joe Pueblo beside him, and he could feel the silent tension that had seized the wagon train, with three exceptions: Bud Denny was plainly full of eager anticipation, Reverend Moreland drove his team with the air of a man going into battle for the Lord, and Judith seemed above it all, her round face quietly happy.

It was dark when they reached the bottom of the stone mountains and he pulled the wagons into a secure spot. He ordered extra sentries to be posted and supper to be quick, the fire put out as soon as they were finished. "We will have our evening hymn service as always," Reverend Moreland pronounced. "Special prayers this night and our voices raised in song."

"Make them short," Fargo said. As the reverend rolled the organ from his wagon and the supper plates were washed and dried, Fargo walked to where Darcy stood stiffly against her wagon. Joe Pueblo dropped back to wait. Darcy's light-brown eyes seemed almost amber as they met him with a cool, waiting stare.

"I suppose I ought to say thanks for what you said back there," she said.

"I was being kind," he told her curtly, and saw her shoulders grow stiff at once.

"Meaning what?" she said.

"Meaning just that. A man experienced in fighting Comanche should have picked up signs. Maybe not the ones I picked up back there, but enough to warn him." She waited, not answering, and he let his voice grow gentler. "Something was wrong, Darcy. I don't know what, but something. Maybe, somehow, someway, your pa got in more than he expected. Or maybe he did get careless. It happens, you know. I think you've got to start facing up to those possibilities."

The tears came into her eyes all at once, but she fought them back with fierceness. "No, I don't care how it looks. He was a fine officer and a wonderful man," she said, paused to draw in a deep breath. "You know what the army pays . . . nothing. You work all your life and you've a lousy little pension. But it was his career. When Pond came along with his offer, Daddy had the leave time coming to him. It was a chance to make some real money for a change, for himself and the six men he took with him. That's all it was, a chance at a good paycheck on his time off. But he wouldn't be careless with other people's lives, not him, never. So you can all go to hell with your theories and accusations."

She brushed past him, strode toward where the others were gathering around Judith at the organ. Fargo watched her lithe, lovely shape move away as Joe Pueblo came up to stand beside him. "Too much love," Joe grunted. "Can't see around it."

"Maybe we're trying too hard to see around it," Fargo said, and Joe frowned. "What's Pond so damn afraid of? That I'll find Colonel Dennison was careless?" Fargo went on. "No, he's afraid of a lot more."

"Where does that leave the colonel?" Joe questioned.

"I don't know. Maybe better," Fargo said.

"And maybe worse," Joe said, and Fargo nodded at the hard truth of it.

Joe went on into the darkness and Fargo took his bedroll down, found a place in the rocks overlooking the wagons. He frowned down for a moment at the knot of figures lingering by the embers of the fire. The hum of their voices signified something less than an argument but more than idle conversation, and he watched until they drifted apart, moving to their wagons in small groups. Only one stayed behind, staring upward as if she could see him. But Henrietta Crown wasn't seeking him, he knew. She was peering up into the night that cloaked Condor Pass. She turned away finally and Fargo lay back and slept. Perhaps the time for answers was drawing close.

6

"Everyone carries a rifle from here on, riding, walking, resting. You eat with it next to you, sleep with it at your side," Fargo told them in the morning as they prepared to pull out. "Joe Pueblo and I will ride point, Smith, Hawkins, Broadman stay close to the last wagon." He saw Bud Denny waiting, his cold eyes too bright. "You ride free but don't get too far from the wagons," he told the man.

He started to swing onto the pinto when Henrietta halted beside him. "When will we get there?" she asked, her intense eyes boring deep into him.

"Maybe by tomorrow night. It'll be slow going now," he said.

She nodded, a strange nod, as if she were digesting a very private piece of information. He watched her climb onto the wagon and take the rifle Amos Alder handed her. She held it upright beside her. Herb and Mary Atkinson passed, his face grave. Mary held a rifle on her lap as if it weren't there. Fargo swung the pinto forward, passed Darcy, who kept her eyes straight ahead. He slowed beside Athena, saw she'd put on a shirt that made her eyes moss-green. Her breasts still curved in a smooth, unbroken line without the hint of a point. He felt a stab of irritation at her.

"You looking pleased with yourself, as if you were going to a damn hoedown," he said.

"Take it as a compliment," she returned. "I don't expect it'll turn out like the last one with you riding trail."

"You expect more than you've a right to," he said curtly.

"It's called being confident," she said tartly.

"It's called being stupid," he returned.

"Can't you ever be nice?" she flared.

"Don't get much reason," he said as he cantered away. He rode ahead, explored the side passages on the right, and let Joe take the ones on the left. He saw the signs, a cholla plant with the lower edges bruised or broken where a horse's legs had brushed it, a moccasined footprint in between two rocks, a lone set of hoofprints hidden in a narrow crevice. Joe would be seeing them on his side, too, he knew, and he rode back to the main passage and the wagons with his jaw set in a grim line. Joe came down and exchanged a silent glance that needed no words.

Fargo called a rest halt a little past the noon hour and Herb Atkinson slid down beside him where he sat against a flat rock. "Any more signs?" the man asked. Fargo saw Athena, nearby, look up at once.

"Enough," Fargo said.

He saw Herb Atkinson's face lengthen. "That means they'll attack, doesn't it?" Herb asked.

"Probably. When they're ready," Fargo said.

Herb rose, his face suddenly almost despairing. He walked slowly back to the others.

"Where?" Fargo heard the question, Athena's voice. "In Condor Pass?"

"That's a good place," he said.

"But what?"

"But the Comanche never does what you expect he'll do," Fargo said.

"Unless it's arranged," Athena said, and the bitterness curled in her voice.

"Maybe not even then," Fargo said.

"No matter, I've enough proof now: Pond's tries to stop us, all the signs you were able to pick up. It proves it couldn't have just happened the way it did unless it was meant to," she said.

"Now all you have to do is live long enough to put together all those pieces that still don't fit," he said, rose, and left her tight-lipped. He swung onto the pinto, saw the others talking earnestly beside the reverend's Conestoga. "Move out," he yelled. "Save it for tonight."

He rode out with Joe Pueblo again and halted to watch as the wagons had trouble on the steep grades, finally called another halt to let the horses get a second wind. He trotted on, glancing back to see another earnest conference taking place, and this time he could hear the reverend's voice raised in prophetlike tones. He halted at a place where the passage leveled off, decided it was as good a place as any to make camp, and waited until the others came along. Scouting the area around the site, he returned, satisfied that it was clear. As he wound his way around from the side, moving through a small space between the rocks, he heard Darcy's voice first, anger and alarm in it, then Bud Denny's arrogant rasp.

Fargo slid from the pinto, made his way on foot through the space, and saw Darcy pinned against a sloping rock, Bud Denny holding her immobile.

"You don't want to act that way, baby," Bud Denny said, and rubbed his chest across Darcy's upturned breasts. "You be nice to me and I'll back you up on anything you want me to say."

"Let me go, damn you," Darcy hissed. "You're hurting me."

"You better start singing another tune. I'll be top dog around here pretty damn soon," Bud Denny said, and tried to press his mouth onto Darcy's lips as she twisted her head away.

Fargo stepped out of the narrow space on the balls of his feet, took three silent strides, and reached the two figures. Bud Denny started to turn, but the Colt came down in a short, scraping blow along the side of his temple. He staggered backward, started to go for his gun, and halted, stared at the barrel of the big Colt. His eyes grew into cold slits as he wiped the trickle of blood from his temple.

"You've got the draw on me," he said.

"That's right. Now get back down with the others," Fargo said. "And don't go near her again."

Bud Denny moved backward. "You'll be payin' for this, Fargo," he growled. "You can count on it."

"When it's time," Fargo said, and holstered the Colt.

Bud Denny turned and disappeared behind the rocks.

"I came up here to get away by myself for a few minutes," Darcy said, straightening her clothes. "He must've followed me."

"No more getting away by yourself. Stay with the wagons," Fargo said coldly.

Darcy started to turn to go down, paused, glanced back at him. "You've seen more signs, Herb said," she slid at him. He nodded, unsmiling. "It doesn't change what I said any," she tossed back, full of bristles at once.

"Didn't expect it would," he said as he walked back to get the pinto and she went on down to the wagons. The dark came quickly and a small fire of mountain brush heated small portions of red beans. Fargo took his plate and sat off by himself in the shadow of Athena's wagon as the others stayed in a small knot. He watched Judith roll the organ down for a short hymn sing and service. The sound would echo through the rock mountain, he knew, but it didn't really matter. There was no point in trying to hide. The reverend had just said his last "amens" when Fargo saw the slender, straight form of

Mary Atkinson moving toward him. She carried the rifle in one hand, the barrel trailing downward.

He rose as she halted before him. Her quiet, church-meeting face lifted to meet his probing glance. "I must talk to you, Mister Fargo," she said softly. "It's about the rifle. You said I should keep thinking about it and get unbothered with it. I tried, but I can't. Herb said I should tell you. He's angered at me."

"Angered?" Fargo echoed.

"He says I'm not pulling my weight, that I'm letting everyone else down. The others all agree with him, even Reverend Moreland," Mary Atkinson said, and a sadness came into her voice.

"Reverend Moreland?" Fargo questioned.

"Yes, I went to him and asked him what was right for me to do."

"What'd the reverend tell you?" Fargo pressed.

"He said it was my duty to use the rifle. He said I should think of myself as a soldier of the Lord," Mary said, and looked apologetic. "Maybe he's right, but I can't do it. I can't fire that rifle to kill anyone. I was raised not to kill. It's written too deep inside me. I can't get it out. That's why Herb told me to come to you. I don't blame him for being angered. I know he's more disappointed in me than anything else. I don't blame any of them. But my pastor back home read the Good Book different than Reverend Moreland. I don't know who's right or wrong."

"You've plenty of company there, Mary," Fargo commented.

"I don't know who to believe anymore or what to do," she said with more sadness than anger.

"Believe in yourself, Mary. Believe in what you feel inside," he said. "And as for what to do, you start tearing up sheets into bandage strips. We may be needing plenty of them." He reached down, gently took the rifle from her hand as she stood very still.

"You're not angered at me, Mister Fargo?" she asked gravely.

"Hell, I've been wondering where we'd get us a nurse," he said. "Just remember to keep your head down." She nodded and he thought he detected a tiny smile flicker in her solemn face. She turned and walked back to the others and it seemed to him that she held her head up just a little higher.

"Damn you, Fargo, you're a barrelhead of mixtures," he heard the voice say and saw Athena emerge from behind the wagon, her eyes round with amazement.

"You objecting?" he asked.

"No, I thought it was wonderful," she said. She started to say more, but he reached out, yanked her to him, and pressed his mouth on hers. She stiffened, pushed her hands against him, but her lips were soft and warm and he forced her mouth open, felt the sweet-cushion taste of her.

"Stop, damn," she gasped, and tore away, the seawater eyes green fire. "What was the idea of that?" she demanded.

He smiled affably. "I knew you'd want to reward a good deed," he said. He left her still sputtering and took his bedroll up into the rocks, slept almost at once. There'd be plenty of time for lying awake.

He found everyone ready to roll when he went down for coffee in the morning. Reverend Moreland, Judith beside him, seemed to be waiting for him. "I'm disappointed in you, Brother Fargo," the reverend said with a benign admonition in his tone.

"Join the line. It's a long one," Fargo said.

"I'm sorry you did not see fit to support my advice to Mary Atkinson," the reverend said. "She needs spiritual remolding."

"Oh, Fargo was just being kind," Judith broke in with a bright smile at the big black-haired man.

"Sometimes it's wrong to be kind," the reverend intoned.

"It's wrong to think you know too damned much," Fargo said, finished his coffee, and strode away. Bud Denny slowed to spear him with hate in his cold eyes. Fargo ignored the man and swung onto the pinto, his glance pausing at Athena just long enough to flash a quick grin. She returned a distant nod and he waved the wagons forward and rode on with Joe Pueblo. The sun reflected from the rocks and sent added heat waves shimmering; Fargo halted as the upward passage flattened out onto a small mountain plateau bordered by rock and strewn with yucca and cholla. His eyes scanned the stone walls and he felt the tingling of his skin, instinct pushing its warning signals at him. He glanced at Joe and saw him nod in the direction of a flat line of rock.

Fargo looked back and saw Athena's wagon struggling slowly into view, Jeff Howard at the reins of the wagon behind her. He rode back, took hold of the cheek strap on the left horse, and guided the team in toward the nearest line of rock, caught Athena's instant frown. He had the others follow in a single line to hug the one side of the small plateau until he called a halt. Bud Denny rode up, scanned the area with a frown. "Everybody out. Dig in behind the wagons," Fargo said. Denny, still scanning the plateau, was the last to ride in behind the wagons. He dismounted, took the rifle from his saddle scabbard.

Fargo watched from the front of Athena's wagon as Joe dismounted beside him. The few minutes began to seem like hours when suddenly the figures appeared, lining up atop the flat rocks first, space between each one. Fargo's eyes were hard as he slowly scanned the line of horsemen, most wearing bear-claw necklaces and headbands to hold back their long, stringy black hair, their faces the high-cheekboned, narrow-eyed dark copper of the Comanche, faces that could have been chiseled out of the rock on which they stood. He counted ten, all with bows, six also carrying lances.

"You thinking what I am?" he said to Joe Pueblo, his mouth finding a grim smile. Joe nodded and lowered himself to the ground, half-hidden behind a wagon wheel. As Fargo watched, the Comanche turned as one, began to move down the opening in the rocks, deliberate and unhurried.

"They take their damn time, don't they?" Jeff Howard muttered.

"When they come out of that opening they'll be riding full out," Fargo said. "They'll come in straight, fire, and turn and go back straight. They present less of a target that way. But we're going to hold fire."

"What?" It was Bud Denny's voice, angry protest spiraling in it.

"Nobody shoots unless I give the order," Fargo said.

"Damn, you're crazy, Fargo," the man threw back.

"Just follow orders, you hear me?" Fargo said, his voice cold steel.

A high-pitched half-scream, half-shout cut off further talk as the Comanche came roaring out of the opening in the rocks, veered to the right, then charged head on.

"Heads down," Fargo yelled as he saw the first volley of arrows fill the air. The shafts thudded into wood and tore through canvas, and Fargo, the Colt in his hand, wriggled alongside Athena, his eyes fastened on the horsemen as they wheeled, came in again. He saw three lances hurtle with death-dealing force. One embedded itself into the reverend's Conestoga and one landed a half-foot from where Amos Alder lay flat with the rifle to his shoulder.

"Hold your fire," Fargo reminded again. The Comanche wheeled in the distance, made another charge, firing their arrows in clusters. They spun away and this time they galloped to the left, racing across the small plateau to disappear into another opening in the rocks.

Fargo waited, let five minutes go by, and then pulled himself to his feet. Denny jumped up instantly. "God-damn, we could've taken at least half of them, maybe all of them," he roared. "What the hell's the matter with you, Fargo?"

"They wanted us to blast away at them," Fargo said quietly. "That was only a testing force. Molokah and his main body of warriors were behind those rocks watching."

"You knew that?" Athena cut in.

"Soon as I saw them. Comanche tactics. First, they wouldn't pick a flat plateau for a full assault. We'd have all the advantages. Second, there were only ten. And last, it's the Comanche way. They're careful. They pretty much know how many of us there are, but they don't know how much rifle power we have or if our womenfolk are going to be shooting or how good we can shoot. They'd have had all those answers if we'd blasted back at them. Now they're still not sure. They still have to be careful."

Fargo moved to the pinto and swung into the saddle. "Let's roll," he said.

"They could be waiting to hit us again?" Athena said.

"Not now. They've had their try. They've gone on now to figure their next move. That's their way," Fargo said. "Start your wagons." He rode out and saw Bud Denny's face still sullen as the man mounted his horse.

"Molokah find out one thing," Joe Pueblo muttered. "He not dealing with some greenhorn wagonmaster."

Fargo's smile was hard. It was a contest he didn't relish and he had to wonder who'd learn the final lesson. He led the wagons on as the small plateau came to an end and they began to crawl up narrow mountain passages again. By the end of the day, the tall arching rock formation lay easily within sight, cutting through the sides of red-brown sandstone. He watched the darkness lower over Condor Pass as the wagons camped in a stone-sided clearing.

He saw Henrietta standing near, her eyes fastened on the great pass as night drew its curtain over it. She turned to him and once again he tried unsuccessfully to see behind the piercing, intense eyes. A terrible cry lay just behind their burning, he decided again, and the woman turned away abruptly, walked to her wagon with a full-bodied sensuousness that could envelope her unexpectedly.

Fargo slowed as he saw Darcy toying with a plate of beef jerky. She glanced at him and looked away, and in her eyes he saw only pain. She seemed to be drawing into herself more and more, erecting a wall of defensiveness for each day's developments. He decided it wasn't time to try to reach her again, and he went on to take his bedroll as the reverend started evening services, Judith playing softly.

Athena met his quick grin as she passed. "I liked that sample last night," he said. "I don't think I'll be waiting much longer to collect the rest of that agreement."

"I said after it's all done with." She frowned.

"I'm changing the rules." He smiled.

"That's not fair," she protested. "I won't agree."

"Be careful or you'll have me believing you," he said, and heard her sharp gasp of anger as he went on.

"You just better believe me, Fargo," she called after him, and he let her hear his laugh as he disappeared into the darkness. He got his bedroll, moved to a spot in the rocks that let him see the wagons through a jagged crevice. He undressed to his shorts as the reverend's service ended and the last notes of the organ faded away. He put his arms behind his head and began to turn over the options that might be his when the sun rose again. He hadn't too many to go over, he pondered unhappily.

A half-moon rose overhead and silhouetted the tops of the rocks. He heard a gecko scurry across a stone behind him and then another sound, soft footsteps just outside where he lay. He sat up, his hand automatically going to the Colt nearby, as the figure appeared in the entranceway between the rocks, a dark shape only, moved forward to become blond-gray hair made silver in the moonlight, a long nightgown cloaking large, heavy breasts. Henrietta Crown stepped to him, sank down on the bedroll, the burning eyes piercing him.

"Surprised, Fargo?" she asked.

"I'd say so," he answered.

"It's not what you're thinking," she said. "Not the heart of it."

"I know that," he said, and saw surprise touch the intense eyes. "You'd have come before now if that's all it was," he said.

"Maybe I'm stronger than most," she said.

He shrugged. "Maybe," he said. "But there's more burning inside you than that."

Her eyes bored into him. "My name's really Henrietta Corn," she said. Fargo frowned, unable to pull memory together quickly enough. "My husband, Henry, was part of the last wagon train. He was massacred at Condor Pass. My two girls, Amy and Beth, were with him," Henrietta said. "Amy was twelve, Beth fourteen." The woman paused again and Fargo waited. "Amy and Beth weren't among the bodies they found. The Comanche took them," she said, leaned forward, the intense eyes flamed with black fire. "I want you to get them back. You can track the Comanche from Condor Pass, the very same ones that are out there waiting now. I want Amy and Beth back. I've money, enough to pay you whatever you want, much more than Athena's paying you for this job."

The woman trembled under the nightgown and Fargo saw the quiver of her large breasts ripple the garment. "Easy, Henrietta," he said gently.

She dismissed his words. "You're going to tell me it

can't be done, but I know it can. You could do it," she said.

"That's not what I was going to tell you," Fargo said, and wondered if he could put the thoughts inside him into words. He'd start gently, he decided. "It's been six months or so since Condor Pass. You don't even know if they're alive," he said.

"They're alive. I know it," Henrietta said.

"Hoping and knowing get all mixed up," Fargo said. She stared at him and her silence was an admission. He reached out, put a hand on her shoulder, chose words as best he could. "The Comanche use up women captives and throw them away," he said. "Sometimes it's best not to find what they've left."

Henrietta's eyes didn't waver. "I've heard sometimes they keep women as special prizes, to show off to other tribes," she said. "Amy and Beth were beautiful blond girls, worth keeping."

Fargo's lips pressed onto each other. "Sometimes they do that," he agreed, paused before finishing. "But they don't keep them untouched."

Henrietta's high-cheekboned face turned away and she stared into the darkness. "I know that, Fargo," she said quietly. "And I want them back. There are all kinds of ways to start a new life in this world. I want my girls back."

"And if they're dead by now?" Fargo asked harshly.

Her eyes met his. "Then I want to know that. Not knowing, wondering, imagining all the worst, I can't live with that any longer. I've got to know." She leaned forward, pressed his arm with her hand. "Whatever you want, I'll pay it. My family has money. I stayed East on family business when Henry and the girls went West. I was to follow them out. You've got to help me, Fargo."

"The money doesn't do it, Henrietta," he said. "I'll have to think on it. Maybe there's a way. Maybe there isn't. Maybe the Comanche will answer it once and for all, for you and for all of us."

"If they don't, I want you to follow them, find Amy and Beth," the woman said, her eyes burning through him. "This is the best chance I'll ever have to find them. That's why I came. I knew this was my one chance."

Fargo let his thoughts race. She was right in her last reasoning. If there was a chance to find her daughters, it would be from Condor Pass. *If.* The word danced in front of him. So many other things were waiting to be answered. He met her burning gaze. "I can't answer you. I'll have to think, to wait and see. That's the best I can do now. I'm sorry," he said. "I'm sorry for all the burning inside you, but I can't put it out."

He felt the line cross his brow as he saw her arms suddenly lift, pull, and the nightdress fly over her head to land on the ground.

"You can put out part of it," she said.

His eyes took in her nakedness, not without surprise, the deep, large breasts with brownish nipples against deep-pink circles. Her skin was unblemished, softly tanned, a layer of extra flesh covering her but giving her a combination of maturity and earthy sensuousness as she rose on her knees before him. Her hips, wide, were beautifully female, the triangle of blackness just below a rounded belly luxuriantly thick. He lifted his gaze to her eyes, saw a new burning inside them.

"I'm not Darcy Dennison," the woman breathed. "I'm not trying to buy. I've lived long enough to know that wouldn't work with your kind of man. I'm just wanting. I've done enough doing without. That's its own burning."

"At the sinkhole, that was you behind the brush," Fargo said.

Henrietta Corn nodded. "I'd left a kerchief and went back to get it when I saw you," she said. "I knew I was through doing without, then."

"What about Amos Alder?" Fargo asked.

She smiled and he realized it was the first time he'd ever seen her smile, wry and rueful as it was. "Maybe another day, another time, when the burning's become human again. Jesus, Fargo, help me," she suddenly cried. She stared at him, put her head back, and her body began to quiver, the large breasts shaking violently. The fire inside her spewed out, beyond ignoring, the burning, wanting so real he could almost feel it, and he saw himself responding, his maleness suddenly flaring into desire.

Henrietta looked down at him and flung herself forward, her body falling onto his, and her skin was surprisingly soft. Her large breasts lifted, pressed into his face. "Jesus, Jesus, Fargo, oh, please, please," she said as she pushed her brownish nipples deep into his mouth. There was no pleading in her gasped cries, no entreaties, only a desperate demand. She fell beside him, her arms locked around his waist and her fleshy thighs wonderfully soft clasps pulling him over her. He thrust into her at once as she rose for him. The sound that came from her was a breathy, almost animal growl—"uuuh . . . uuuh . . . uuh . . . aaagh . . . aaaagh"—deepening with his every thrust.

She was large and opened wide, flowing wetly around him as she rose with her every movement, no tender wanting but an obliterating totality of desire, her gasps growled noises, almost bearlike. "More, more . . . aaagh . . . ah . . . ah . . ." she began to chant, pressing him to her, rubbing her breasts into his face. He felt himself being swept along, growing as animallike as she, and he moved harshly into her, driving deep and powerfully; and she only growled out for more and suddenly he felt her seem to go through a sudden spasm as her arms fell outward, he legs opened, and then she flung herself upward, carrying him high on her pelvis and the shaking of her body made him cling onto her hips with his hand. The growl turned into a guttural rasp and died away in a frenzy of grunting gasps as she fell back onto the bedroll, to tremble quietly.

He drew from her and she stared at him as if in a trance, slowly focusing on his face. "Jesus, oh, Fargo, oh, God," she said, pushed her pillowy soft breasts into his face. "Again, please, again," she breathed.

He nodded, his eyes taking in the very real beauty of her, a mature, female beauty with a body made of its own wisdoms and skin as soft as a sixteen-year-old's. And the burning, the terrible, devouring hunger that was a thing of excitement, that allowed for no denying, no holding back. "Oh, Jesus, Fargo," she cried out suddenly, sitting up as if an explosion had gone off inside her, and perhaps it had. She fell upon his throbbing maleness, brought her body half over his, rubbed him into the hollow of her breasts, across her nipples, then fell upon him with warm, enveloping lips. The low growling began at once again. "Uuuh . . . uuuh . . . oooh, Jesus, oh . . . oh . . . aaah . . . ah . . . aaaah," as she pulled and caressed and exulted in the touch and taste and feel of him. She pulled away abruptly, each move as if another switch had gone on inside her, and she rubbed her thick triangle back and forth over him, thrust herself onto him, and cried out a throaty rasp of ecstasy.

This time when she exploded she quivered hard against him as if she could somehow force herself inside his skin, and his hands clasped around her buttocks as she stayed with him until finally she lay back, the staring again in her eyes. Finally she brought her focus back to his face and she took his head in both hands, cradled him against her breasts, a sudden kind of sensual motherliness. She drew away finally, rubbed her hands down her face. Fargo watched the way her pillowy breasts swayed with her every movement and again he admired the earthy sensuousness that was Henrietta Corn. It wasn't just the burning. It was there inside her, a deep passion that was forged out of love and pain and her own being. She leaned the large breasts over his chest and her intense eyes searched his face.

"Surprised, Fargo?" she asked. No girlish coyness but a woman's right to know in her eyes.

"Yes," he said honestly. "You're a rare woman, Henrietta."

She almost smiled as she drew the nightgown on, and he was sorry to see her full-fleshed beauty vanish beneath the garment. He stood up with her and her dark-fire eyes still burned. "A night I'll remember," she said.

"I damnwell will, too," he told her.

"But I must have the other, Fargo," she said. "You must help me with the other."

His smile held ruefulness and honesty. "This was the easy part," he said.

She pressed close to him for a moment and left then, looking back only once, all the words in the deep burning of her eyes.

Fargo stretched out on the bedroll and cursed Ellsworth Pond. The rotten bastard had destroyed a wagon train and so much more. Somehow, someway, he had done it, and the reasons still eluded definition. There was still no motive, no real explanation for what had happened or why. There were still only answers that failed to explain the heart of it. It was a sentence where all the words seemed to fit, but they made no meaning. He turned on his side. Dawn was only a few hours away.

7

Their eyes were as one, fixed on the towering rock arches of Condor Pass as they glistened in the light of the early sun. Fargo sat the pinto with the outriders behind him, his glance moving from wagon to wagon. Henrietta's intense eyes seemed to leap time and distance as they stared at Condor Pass. There was excitement in Athena's face; she'd put on a yellow shirt as if for the ocassion. Maybe facing death ought to be festive, Fargo reflected. Darcy sat grimly, the pride and the growing uncertainty inside her struggling in her eyes. The others held mostly fear in their faces, Reverend Moreland's righteous expression more a mask than a shield. Beside him, Judith's round face was suddenly less round, little lines of tension pulling at her mouth.

"You'll be reaching the entrance to the path in a half-hour," Fargo told them. "If everything is all right, we'll be waiting there for you."

"And if you're not?" Abe Sprain asked.

"Don't go through," Fargo said as he wheeled the pinto around and started up the passageway at a fast trot. Joe Pueblo followed, Bud Denny and the other outriders close behind. Fargo pulled up when he reached the beginning of Condor Pass, motioned to the others to dismount. His eyes were blue quartz as they moved across the towering arch of rocks on both sides.

He saw nothing and the pass lying ahead of him was filled with a tomblike silence that seemed entirely appropriate. He started for the arching wall on the right, motioned for Bud Denny and Hawkins to follow him, and Joe made off for the opposite side with Broadman and Smith behind him.

Fargo moved on surefooted steps as he clambered up the rocks, the Colt in his hand, leaping lightly from stone to stone, pausing to sink down every few moments and let his eyes sweep the area ahead. It was made of creviced rock and jagged spears of wind-carved sandstone, hiding places, each of them. Too many hiding places, he grunted. But the arching rock formation remained still and empty as he made his way forward in short, darting bursts. He had Denny and Hawkins cover him as he climbed over an exposed area, flattened himself into a stone niche on the other side, and surveyed the top of the formation. Nothing moved, glistened, sounded, and he moved forward to the edge of the arch where he could peer down into the pass.

He'd gone almost halfway above the pass and Joe Pueblo was somewhere across from him, he knew. He let his glance sweep the opposite arch of rock and glimpsed a figure, Smith, scurrying hunched over between two peaks of stone. Fargo peered forward across the remainder of the arched formation on his side, then across to the other side. He was high enough to command a good view now, high enough to see the Comanche if they were waiting. They'd have to be positioned low enough to sweep down on the pass and close enough to pour fire down onto the wagons, and they were not there. He grunted grimly, rose to stand straight for a moment, and knew Joe would spot him and know what the gesture meant. He turned and began to climb back the way they'd come, picking up Bud Denny and Hawkins along the way.

Joe and the other two men were just coming down

from the other side when he reached the mouth of the pass where he'd left the horses. Joe Pueblo met his gaze with a harsh half-laugh. "He knew you'd expect him in the pass," Joe said.

"So he decided to wait somewhere else." Fargo nodded.

"Where?" Bud Denny asked.

Fargo shrugged. "Somewhere on the other side of the pass. I don't know the lay of the land there. Bastard," Fargo bit out harshly. "He's letting us commit ourselves so we can't turn back or hold off." He grunted in bitter admiration and swung onto the pinto as Athena's wagon came into view.

Bud Denny mounted his horse, halted beside him for a moment. "I'm calling you as soon as it's over," the man said, his hand moving to touch the side of his temple. "You better be ready."

"If we're both still standing," Fargo said, and moved on to meet Athena's wagon. He waved her forward and swung Darcy's wagon alongside hers, lined the others up in twos as they entered Condor Pass. The eerie feeling enveloped him and he knew the others felt it even more so, the tomblike silence broken only by the sound of the wagon wheels. No one spoke and he glanced back at Henrietta. She stared forward as her hands gripped the edge of the wagon seat so hard her knuckles were drawn of blood. Darcy stared straight head, the thin cords of her neck throbbing. Athena had lost her look of eagerness and her eyes had turned a dark and troubled blue.

They rode with unseen companions, each of them, Condor Pass a silent passage of bitterness. Fargo moved out in front of the wagons, trotted the pinto onto the high point of the pass, and reined up abruptly, his mouth becoming a hard, thin line. Joe Pueblo came up beside him as he stared at the remains of the six wagons, smashed, skeletal remains, each one standing separate, as though they were crude, jagged tombstones. Monuments to death . . . and to what else, he wondered. Deceit, treachery, stupidity? To greed and error? Or to planned, deliberate murder? He swung from the pinto and started for the wagons. Their smashed, uncharred presence one more enigma among all the others, but they seemed to wait frozen in place, as if offering silent answers that could now fall into place.

He felt his pace hurrying and Joe Pueblo caught up to him as he reached the first wagon, circled it, his eyes scanning the splintered sides and smashed floorboards. He hurried on to the next and the wagon nearest that one. His eyes met Joe Pueblo's narrowed glance and Joe nodded. Fargo saw the figure moving at the other side, Henrietta, going from wagon to wagon, suddenly halting, her hand reaching in to pick a limp torn doll from inside the wreckage. *Damn,* he swore silently and watched Henrietta's face as she held the doll, stared at it, and he saw her lips quiver. He looked away to see Athena coming toward him, Darcy quickly following.

"What are you looking for?" Athena asked.

"Answers," he said, and she waited. "I found some," he went on, pointed to the smashed bottom of the wagon. "False bottoms, every wagon had one," he said. "That's why Pond provided everyone with one of his own new wagons."

He saw Athena's eyes grow round. "False bottoms?" she echoed. "For what?"

He shrugged. "Pond was smuggling something," he said, his eyes going to the splintered false floor of the wagon again. "Rifles, I'd guess," he said.

"To whom?" Athena frowned.

"To the Comanche," Fargo said grimly.

Darcy's voice sounded. "That's another guess, of course," she said.

"There's not much guessing to it anymore," Fargo said quietly. "The Comanche knew the rifles were there.

That's why they didn't burn the wagons as they usually do."

Darcy's face clouded in protest. "He could've been shipping them someplace else and the Comanche found out and attacked," she offered.

"It doesn't come out right," he said. "If that was it, your pa would have looked for and picked up Comanche signs. But we know he didn't. He led the wagons into the pass here for Sunday services because he knew the Comanche were going to be here waiting."

"So he could get himself and everyone else massacred? That's ridiculous," Darcy flung back.

Fargo drew a deep breath made of frustration and grimness. "No, I don't think your pa expected he and the others to be massacred. He was crossed up or something else went wrong."

"You're still saying he was into gunrunning with Ellsworth Pond, and that's a lie. He wouldn't do that," Darcy protested.

"I'm saying only one thing, dammit," Fargo exploded. "The whole wagon train was a clever cover Pond set up to smuggle guns to the Comanche. The rest of the pieces are still missing and only two men know the answers, Molokah and Ellsworth Pond." He paused, drew in a deep breath. "One of them's waiting for us right now. Let's not keep him waiting too long," he said.

He turned, strode to where Henrietta leaned against the smashed wagon, the limp doll held to her breast. Her eyes met his gaze as he gently pried the doll from her fingers, put it back into the wagon. The question burned from her stare and he nodded. There were still answers to find. He'd add one more. Maybe it was the only one that really mattered. He took her by the arm and brought her back to her wagon.

Athena's eyes followed him as he climbed onto the pinto, her brow furrowed. "How did she know that doll would be in that wagon?" she asked.

"She knew," Fargo snapped.

"You're not telling me something," Athena prodded.

"Another cigar," he snapped, and Athena started to press further, her lips parted, when she saw his eyes and pulled words back. He turned the blue-quartz gaze from her and cantered off, his chiseled face pulled tight as he waved the wagons forward.

Joe Pueblo beside him, Fargo started down the other side of Condor Pass, the incline a gradual one, and his eyes moved ceaselessly back and forth from each bordering stone arch. But there was only a mocking silence and he pressed forward. The pathway grew narrower and he saw the pass coming to an end in a narrow bottleneck wide enough for only one wagon at a time. He sent the pinto into a trot through the bottleneck and saw the land widen on the other side, but only enough for two wagons abreast. Fargo reined to a halt as Joe rode up. The land continued to slope gently downward, and at the other end he saw a wall of stone, the pathway turning sharply to the right at the wall. It made the stretch into a kind of box canyon, but it was the two sides that held Fargo's interest. The right side was a sheer sandstone wall only a fly could negotiate, but on the left the rock formation rose and fell, honeycombed with narrow passageways and jagged slabs.

Fargo's lips pulled into a thin smile made of grimness and he saw Joe nod at the honeycombed rocks, agreement in the gesture. It was the made-to-order place, the wagons committed to going forward out of the pass with no room to turn around, not even room to form a circle. "They figure to wait till we're strung out and come charging out of those rocks at us," Fargo said.

Joe Pueblo nodded agreement again and Fargo uttered a silent curse. His eyes became blue slits as he peered down the boxlike canyon, the far end not really very far away at the base of the incline. He glanced back as Athena's wagon began to come through the narrow bottleneck out of Condor Pass and he spun his eyes back to the honeycombed rocks at the side of the canyon. The Comanche chief had used the hunter's wisdom: wait till the prey is committed to a move, a path of flight. Wait till there is neither place to hide nor time to make another move. Fargo's eyes returned to the far end of the canyon again as his thoughts raced. Commitment was a two-way street, hunter as well as prey bound by it. The hunter's strike, once launched, was also beyond changing. Fargo let his thoughts take on words.

"Once he attacks, he's got to keep on and he's got only one way to attack," he said. "He's got to come out of those rocks into the open, into the center of the canyon." Joe's nod was puzzled. "First, we don't try to make a run for it. We don't string ourselves out as he figures we'll do. We bunch up here at this end to concentrate firepower. Second, a cross fire in this place, with him in the middle, could cut him to pieces. Five, even four men at the other end would be enough to do it."

"They have to get down there," Joe snorted. "And have cover when they get there. He'd cut them down before they got halfway there."

"The world is full of surprises." Fargo smiled. He turned the pinto and waved Athena on a few yards, pulled her to a halt. "Bring your wagon alongside," he told Darcy. Joe guided the others as they came, lining them up two abreast almost directly behind one another. Fargo rode up and down the grouping, grunted in satisfaction. It was deep enough and concentrated enough. "Take cover beneath the wagons," he ordered. "Break out all the ammunition you've got. It's showdown time."

He swung from the pinto, led the horse to the far side of the wagons as Bud Denny and Hawkins dismounted. "Pick a spot under the wagons. Form rows behind one another," Fargo instructed the others, "and try to fire in volleys." He lay down beside Athena, saw Darcy on her stomach, a rifle held to her shoulder. The others had positioned themselves and he met Henrietta's glance for an instant, went on, searched for Mary Atkinson, and finally found her lying flat, a roll of bedsheet strips beside her.

"I don't see anything at all," Athena said, and ended the sentence with a sharp gasp of breath drawn in. Fargo peered from below the wagon to see the line of horsemen suddenly etched on top of the rocks. He guessed perhaps thirty, and his eyes moved across the figures. He swore silently as he saw that most carried rifles. He halted his glance at the figure at the far end, a lance in one hand, a rifle in the other. The man sat the horse as if he were a transplanted pine tree, a narrow, long-waisted figure wearing only a breechclout, long arms made of steel sinews. But it was the chief's face that held him, all harsh angles made harsher by a cruel slit of a mouth and eyes that seemed to be black light, wild, fevered eyes made of hate. It was a face, once seen, never to be forgotten. As he watched, Molokah raised the lance, held it high for a moment, then plunged his long, sinewy arm downward. The horsemen disappeared from view and Fargo pressed his cheek against the stock of the heavy Sharps rifle.

"Get ready," he warned. "They'll probe with their first rush, then go back and regroup. After that they'll keep coming in waves." He saw Bud Denny with Smith at the edge of Darcy's wagon, his lips pulled back in eager anticipation. Another minute passed and suddenly the canyon erupted with a wild shout and the thudding of unshod Indian ponies. The honeycombed rocks seemed to come alive as the Comanche warriors poured out of the creviced passages at full gallop. They were in the center of the flat incline in seconds, wheeling their horses to charge toward the bunched wagons. Rifle fire and arrows ripped into the wagons and Fargo drew a bead on one attacker, missed as the Indian swerved. He heard the burst of return fire from beneath the wagons, a clustered volley, and he nodded in approval, grazed another Comanche's shoulder as the man skidded his pony in a tight circle. The Indians fired from low on their horses and whirled to race back into the rocks. He saw two with red-streaked bodies that nonetheless rode perfectly.

"Anyone hit?" he called out.

"No," Jeff Howard said after a moment.

Fargo leaped to his feet and motioned to Joe Pueblo. "Sprain and Howard, you come with me," he called as he ran to the rear of the reverend's Conestoga. "Get that organ down," he ordered. As the square pump organ rolled from the wagon, he saw Judith push to her feet, her round face filling with fervor.

"Yes, of course, of course," she cried out as she ran toward him. "How wonderful. The Lord's songs to fill our hearts with His strength. 'Onward, Christian Soldiers.' " She halted in front of him, her face shining, and she threw a glance back at the reverend, who peered uncertainly from under the wagon. "You see, Mister Fargo is a God-fearing man. I told you so," she said.

"Right now he's a Comanche-fearing man," Fargo hissed as he and Joe began to roll the organ forward. "Get the hell out of the way."

Judith stepped aside, the frown taking over her face. "What are you doing?" she asked.

"We're going to have a different kind of hymn sing," he threw back as they rolled the organ between the wagons. He brought it to a stop as they reached the front line of Conestogas, and he crouched down behind the flat rear side of the organ, Joe Pueblo lining up behind him. Sprain and Howard fitted themselves behind the rest of the organ, one hand holding their rifles, the other against the organ.

"Stay in tight and keep pushing till we reach the

other end. It's downhill and this thing's on rollers. Don't try to fire back. Just keep your head down and push," Fargo said.

"No," he heard the anguished cry, Judith's voice, and she rushed forward to clutch at his arm. "You can't. You'll destroy it," she protested.

"We're going to make beautiful music," he growled, cast a glance at Athena, who had pulled herself up on one elbow. The slightly smug, wry satisfaction in her eyes needed no words and he tossed a quick grin at her. "One more cigar," he said and then, calling over his shoulder to the others, "*PUSH!*" The organ rolled forward with ease, gathering speed quickly on the gradual incline. The Comanche would watch in confusion and perplexity for a moment, he was certain, enough time for the organ to reach the halfway point. He was right by a yard when the little canyon erupted in a volley of rifle fire and a hail of arrows from the rocks.

Fargo ducked lower as he pressed forward in a crouching run, his body pushed hard against the side of the organ. He heard the bullets smashing into the instrument, sharp, wood-splintering sounds, the arrows landing with a thudding vibration, and with it the sound of pipes and reeds shattering in a series of small pinging and groaning noises. A scream rang out from behind them, Judith Moreland's voice, drowned out by another volley of shots that slammed into the instrument. The sound of the keyboard being blasted away was a sudden tinkling noise above the gunshots. A half-dozen bullets tore out through the back of the organ and Fargo felt one graze the top of his head. But they were only a few yards from the end of the little canyon, the wall directly ahead of them.

"Swing it around," he yelled back, pressed his shoulder hard against the front of the instrument, and felt the organ swinging, coming to a halt with the front facing out. He dropped to the ground as another volley smashed out the back top panel of the instrument to open a small, splintered window. "Thanks," he muttered as he poked the Sharps through the hole. Jeff Howard had room to poke his rifle through beside him and he saw Sprain and Joe Pueblo flattened behind the corners of the organ.

The rocks erupted again as the Comanche poured out. They wheeled, raced toward the wagons. "Fire," Fargo yelled, and picked off one of the horsemen. He seemed to leap upward in exuberance as the shot blasted a hole just below the back of his neck. The cross fire poured in with deadly accuracy and Fargo saw the Comanche veer away from the wagons, turn, and start to race back toward the organ. He saw Joe Pueblo duck back as a flurry of shots kicked up the ground. But the Comanche were toppling on all sides as the wagons poured volley upon volley into them from their end.

The Indians veered away, turned, milled in a circle, and Fargo glimpsed the tall straight form racing out of the rocks with another dozen warriors. Molokah charged into the center of his horsemen, shouting, waving the lance, and Fargo saw the Comanche wheel again, reform instantly. They raced toward the wagons in full gallop and Fargo stepped from behind the organ, began to fire the Sharps as fast as it could shoot. Molokah had chosen to try to overrun the wagons in an all-out attack, ignoring the return fire from the small force beneath the Conestogas. But the cross fire was a deadly hail that refused ignoring. "Faster, dammit, pour it into them," Fargo shouted, firing off another round, feeding bullets into the rifle with one hand as he fired with the other.

He saw the Comanche falter, only a handful still on their ponies as they reached the front row of wagons, and half of those toppled to the ground. He saw the tall form wheel away, race to the rocks, and the others break off to follow. The Comanche chief disappeared into the first opening in the rocks, the ragged string of followers moving after him. Fargo lowered the Sharps and drew in a deep draft of air. He glanced at the others. Joe Pueblo and Howard straightened up, but he saw Abe Sprain holding one hand to his left shoulder where a circle of red soaked his shirt.

"Bad?" Fargo asked quickly.

"Hurts bad, but it passed through. I felt it tear out of my shoulder blade," Sprain said. Howard put an arm under him for support; Fargo paused, took in the silence that had descended with startling suddenness. He glanced at the organ, a shattered, splintered box, the keyboard torn away, its innards caved to one side, the one end hanging half off.

"Damn good organ," he muttered as he started forward. Joe Pueblo fell in beside him and he realized his shirt was soaked through with perspiration. He picked his way up the canyon past the litter of lifeless Comanche bodies and he saw figures pulling themselves out from under the bullet-riddled, arrow-studded wagons. "The cross fire," he muttered to Joe Pueblo. "They'd have overrun us easy without the cross fire."

Joe nodded silent agreement as they reached the wagons. Fargo's eyes swept the scene and grew grim. Athena leaned against the wheel of her wagon, her face made of horror and aftershock. Darcy sat with her head buried into her hands and Fargo's eyes halted where Herb Atkinson knelt beside a still, silent form, staring with vacant eyes. Mary Atkinson still looked at though she were going to a church meeting, Fargo noted bitterly, let his eyes move on. Henrietta Corn wrapped clothes around Amos Alder's leg and her eyes met his quick glance. He saw Hawkins holding his arm, waiting for Henrietta to get to him, moved his eyes on again. There'd be no need to apologize to Judith about the organ; he saw her round form lying half over the reverend's. Broadman and Smith each had a half-dozen arrows sticking up from their still bodies and Fargo lifted his eyes to see Bud Denny standing just outside the wagon.

He met Bud Denny's eyes, saw they were bright with excitement, and he still held the six-gun in his hand. "I must've got me a round dozen," he said.

Fargo stared at the younger man, saw the wild enjoyment of killing in Bud Denny's eyes, and felt a towering disgust rising inside him. He started to turn away when Bud Denny's voice rose. "We got some settling to do, Fargo," the man said. "I'm calling you."

"Haven't you had enough killing?" Fargo said, looking back at the man. "Just look around you, for God's sake."

"You're scared Fargo." Bud Denny laughed. "I always knew it."

"Answer me, dammit," Fargo demanded.

Bud Denny's mouth was a line of twisted arrogance, his eyes made of unfeeling cruelty. "Shit, killin's fun," he said. Fargo saw his jaw tighten, his eyes grow hard. "I'm waitin', Fargo," he growled.

Fargo felt contempt mix with the grim fury inside him. Bud Denny was not only a warped, twisted killer, but he was happy to give himself the unfair edge. He had his gun in hand, held at his side, his finger already on the trigger. Fargo drew a deep sigh, seemed about to turn away, and saw the frown touch Bud Denny's brow. When his hand moved, it was too fast to follow, the Colt snapping from the holster and the shot exploding all in one motion. Bud Denny's hand hadn't reached his waist as the bullet smashed into the center of his chest. His eyes focused on the big black-haired man in front of him as he started to pitch forward. There was only one expression in the cold orbs: utter and total surprise. It was still there as he fell, to lay stretched out on the ground.

"Fun's over," Fargo murmured as he turned away. He walked to the pinto and swung into the saddle, glanced at Jeff Howard. "Have Hawkins and Abe help you with the burying," he said, saw Athena come out of her trance.

"Where are you going?" she asked.

"To get some answers," he said, and met Henrietta's eyes. "You coming?" he asked Joe, and the Indian swung onto the gelding. Fargo rode off briskly, made his way into the honeycombed rocks, and easily picked up the trail.

"You want to fill me in?" Joe asked blandly.

"Molokah's got to have a camp not too far away," Fargo said. "If we're going to finish him, this is the time. He's hurting and he hasn't got more that half-a-dozen warriors left."

"That's so," Joe agreed. "But you talk about answers back there."

"Molokah can fill in the missing pieces on Condor Pass," Fargo said. "But there's something else." As Joe listened, he told about Henrietta and her girls. "Maybe something good will come out of this yet," he said when he finished.

"Maybe," Joe said as they rode on in silence. The Comanche had made no attempt to hide their tracks. They were in flight and didn't expect to be followed, anyway. The purple gray of dusk slid over the land as Fargo rode into a hilly terrain with a stand of shadbush spreading over the ground. It was almost dark when he reined up on the top of a rise to peer down at a line of piñon pine growing in a half-circle around a small cluster of tepees. He dismounted at once, squatted down, and waited for darkness.

"Squaws," Joe Pueblo remarked. "They get ready to cry for dead around fire."

"Let's get in closer," Fargo said as the darkness came. He led the pinto down into the stand of piñon pine, left the horse, and moved in a wolflike loping crouch to the edge of the pines. The Comanche camp lay directly in front of him, the squaws already gathered around a small fire. Joe had just settled down beside him when he saw a short, old squaw herd the two slender figures from one of the tepees. Fargo saw the long blond hair at once, watched as the two girls moved nearer the firelight. Each carried a bundle of wood that they placed on the fire under the old squaw's direction. When the taller girl placed a twig in the wrong place she received a slap across the side of the head from the old squaw.

Fargo studied the two girls as they moved around the circle, their faces still unlined, still unmarked, their dresses tattered, the taller girl's young, full breasts showing through the tears in her dress. Only their eyes, half-staring, seeing with a deadened glaze, told that they had not been treated as untouchable prizes. As the women around the fire began to moan, their voices rising in an eerie chant, half-cry and half-song, the squaw shepherded the two girls back into the tepee and took up a position in front of the flap. Fargo felt Joe nudge his arm and he glanced over to see Molokah stepping from another tepee. The Comanche stood alone, his tall, slender form motionless as the fevered, black-fire eyes scanned the camp. But there was defeat in the long, cruel face and the Comanche seemed almost lost, staring blankly at the women and then lifting his eyes to the dark sky. He sank down on his knees and began to chant along with the women.

Four warriors appeared from deeper in the camp, standing silently over the wailing women. They remained as Molokah rose to his feet and retreated into his tepee. Joe Pueblo's whisper was barely audible. "He's alone. We can take him," he said. "Or the girls."

Fargo's eyes grew distant for a long moment. "The girls," he murmured. "You stay here and cover me if anything goes wrong." He stayed crouched, moved to one side, dropped to his stomach, and began to crawl along the edge of the piñon pines, inching his way around the perimeter of the camp.

The wailing of the squaws became a welcome sound, letting him move with less fear or noise. He reached the tepee where the squat old crone stood guard outside, worked his way forward to the back of the canvas. He halted, lifted the bottom an inch, felt it give, raised it farther, enough to slide his body inside. He halted halfway in on his belly, raised his head to see the two girls staring at him, starting to get to their feet. He put a finger to his lips and pushed the rest of his body into the tepee, lifted himself to his feet at once. The older girl, Beth, had her arm around Amy's shoulder and both stared at him with frozen disbelief, the residue of hopelessness. A tiny fire glimmered in one corner of the tepee. Again, he put his finger to his lips and pointed to the canvas at the back circle of the tepee.

Amy, the younger one, was the first to move, darting away from her sister to drop to her knees by the edge of the canvas. She curled her fingers around the bottom of the tepee, began to lift, flattening herself to crawl under. Beth threw another glance of disbelief at him and crossed the tepee to drop to the ground beside her sister. Fargo moved to follow them, waited as Beth's form began to crawl beneath the edge of the canvas. He started to drop to his knees when he heard the canvas flap come open and looked up to see the Comanche warrior enter. He saw the man's eyes dart across the empty tepee, fasten on him.

The Comanche wore a tomahawk in his waistband, but his first move was to shout the alarm. "Shit!" Fargo swore as the man's voice reverberated inside the tepee. The Colt was in his hand, firing, as the Comanche reached for his tomahawk. Fargo didn't wait to see the shot slam into the man's abdomen. With another curse, he dived under the tepee, pulled himself out the other side. Beth and Amy stood clutching each other in terror and Fargo heard the shouts from the camp, running footsteps, and then Joe's six-gun firing, three shots, then two more. The squaws screamed and the running footsteps vanished.

Fargo grasped Beth's hand, yanked her into the piñon pines after him, ran to where he saw Joe backing into the trees, reloading to fire off another three shots. "Got five of them," Joe said as Fargo reached him. "Didn't see any others."

The sound came from behind him, branches being flung aside, and Fargo glimpsed the tall form moving like a dark wraith through the pines. He pushed the girls at Joe. "Get to the horses with them. Be ready to ride if I don't make it," he said, took a moment to watch Joe vanish into the dark of the piñons with the two girls, and then he whirled, eyes peering into the trees. The tall form had vanished and Fargo brought his Colt up, slowly made a circle as he crouched, paused every half-turn to listen. But the Comanche knew how to move with silent steps, Fargo grunted to himself, slowly turned again. A faint noise spun him around and he fired and cursed himself for overanxiousness. He dropped to one knee, his ears straining, edged beside one of the thinnish trunks. A sudden spray of dirt scattered along the ground, and he whirled, realized too late that it had been tossed by hand, started to spin back and saw the lance hurtling at his face. He managed to pull his face to the side and the lance smashed into the tree, grazing his jaw. The heavy pole dropped enough to smash into his shoulder, catching a nerve end, and he felt his arm grow numb, the Colt slip from his fingers.

He saw the tall figure leap out of the darkness, a wide knife glinting for an instant in an upraised hand, and Fargo dived sideways and felt the rush of air over his head as the knife came down in a wide arc. He rolled and his right arm tingled with the numbness. He tried to flex it and it refused to obey. The Comanche chief came at him again and Fargo rolled backward again and came up on his feet. Molokah flung a curse at him, followed with a stream of words, and Fargo failed to catch even a single phrase. The Comanche spoke a dialect of the Shoshonean language, too different from Sioux or Algonquin to pick up. Fargo crouched, circled, and saw the Comanche feint, rush in with an upward thrust of the knife. Fargo flung himself backward, landed against a tree trunk, held here for a moment. Molokah leaped in to plunge the knife deep and Fargo dropped almost to his knees. He heard the blade slam into the tree as he lifted his left fist in an uppercut, drove it upward with all the force of his powerful shoulder muscles.

It smashed into the point of the Comanche's chin and the long, narrow form staggered backward, dropped to one knee. The Comanche shook his head to clear it, looked up too late to avoid the kick. Fargo's foot landed along the side of his jaw and Fargo heard the sound of bone cracking. The long body toppled sideways, quivered for an instant, and then Molokah half-rose and Fargo saw the knifeblade still clutched in the man's hand. He tried to move his right arm again, but the numbness refused to go away. He started toward the Comanche but Molokah was pulling himself to his feet, the knife held in front of him.

Fargo saw the tall body tense, lunge forward, bringing the knife upward to rip at his belly. He could only twist away and the Comanche whirled instantly, swung the blade in a flat arc, and again Fargo had to fall backward. Molokah's jaw had already begun to swell out of shape, he saw, but the Comanche was beyond feeling pain. Rage consumed his tall, sinewy body, the kind of fury no mere blows could subdue. Fargo moved backward, swung his arm, and it moved, the numbness all but gone. He backpedaled again as Molokah advanced, his long arms waving, feinting, suddenly stabbing out, sending the knife in a flat arc. Fargo continued to move backward as he circled, ducked under a long, slashing blow, and tensed the muscles of his right arm. He felt the power flow through them once again and he stepped forward, let the knife slash within inches of his face, twisted to one side, and struck before the Indian could bring his long arm back to slash again. The blow smashed into the now-misshapen, broken jaw, and Fargo felt the jawbone come unhinged.

Molokah staggered backward, his jaw hanging open. The blow would have sent an ordinary man into senselessness, pain blotting out all else. But the Comanche came forward again, long arms sweeping the air with slashing blows, and once again Fargo gave ground. He had come full circle, found himself beside the tree where the lance still hung with point embedded. He leaped forward, drew Molokah off balance as the man lashed out with the knife, regained balance to meet Fargo's counterblow. But the Trailsman spun, seized the lance with both hands, and yanked it free.

Molokah swung around the tree trunk and Fargo dived forward as the knife grazed the back of his neck. He fell to his knees, twisted onto his back, and the Comanche, wild man's eyes behind his misshapen, hang-jawed gargoyle's face, leaped in for the kill. Fargo swung the lance up, thrust it forward, and Molokah saw the pointed blade, his eyes rolling backward, but he was beyond stopping his leap. He came down onto the lance with the force of all his raging fury, and Fargo felt the shock waves travel up his arms as he held the lance steady. The tall figure dangled atop it, long arms and legs waving, not unlike a giant insect on the end of a collector's pin.

Fargo grimaced as he drew on all his strength to throw the lance and its grisly captive to the side. He watched as the Comanche chief landed on his back, his hands grasping the lance, a futile effort to pull it free, and then they fell away and the long body quivered violently and lay still. Fargo pulled himself to one knee, rested, hung his arms down, and let the strength creep back into muscles and tendons. He saw the Colt beside the tree, picked it up, pushed it into his holster, and stood up, swayed for a moment, and shook dizziness from his head. He started forward, falling into his long, loping stride in a few moments. The piñon pines thinned out and he saw the two horses, headed for them. Joe Pueblo sat the gelding, Amy in front of him. Beth waited on the Ovaro and Fargo halted before climbing into the saddle.

"Ready to give up on me?" he asked.

"No," Joe answered. "It seem like long time to you?"

Fargo pulled himself into the saddle behind the girl. "Like a lifetime," he said, and moved the pinto forward.

A small fire burned beside the silent wagons when they reached the little canyon and the dawn was only hours away. He saw Henrietta stand up, take a step forward as he halted the pinto and let the girl slide to the ground. Her eyes bored into Beth, then into Amy as both girls stood as if frozen. Henrietta's arms opened and she took another step forward and then the two girls were clinging to her, trembling, pressed tight against her. There were no words. There were none needed. The words would come later. He watched Henrietta turn, move to the wagon with the two girls in her arms. She let them climb into the wagon first, paused to turn her eyes to where Fargo watched from the saddle. The burning was gone from them; he smiled, and again there were no words needed.

Fargo swung to the ground and saw Athena, the robe around her shoulders. "She told me about the girls after you left," Athena said.

Fargo nodded, met Athena's eyes. "No questions, no

talk, nothing. See me, come morning," he said as he pulled his bedroll down and made his way to a spot just beyond the wagons. He undressed, pulled the blanket around himself, and exhaustion enveloped him at once and he slept with body, mind, and spirit drained.

8

The morning sun was full and he heard the others stirring behind the wagons when he woke. He lay resting a little longer, finally rose, used his canteen to wash. Dressed, he joined the others and saw Henrietta first. She had put on a white blouse with pink flowers embroidered on it and it said all there was to say. She pressed her hand into his for a brief moment and saw the question in his eyes. "They wanted to stay in the wagon," she said. "It'll take a long time." A tiny smile stole the soberness from her face. "But I've plenty of that," she added.

"Are you going on?" Fargo asked.

"Yes. Amos will go with us," she said. She cast a glance across to where Abe Sprain and Jeff Howard looked on. "Abe and Jeff are going on, too," she said, and Fargo saw both men nod agreement.

"We figure there's no reason not to," Abe said. "We'll travel together."

"You won't be having trouble from here on now," Fargo said.

"I'm riding with these folks," Hawkins said, his arm bandaged. "Maybe find a better life for myself. I figure I've used up all my luck on this trip."

Fargo's eyes moved on, found Herb Atkinson leaning against his wagon, loss and pain wreathing his face as he stared at the ground. Fargo half-turned, to see Athena step forward, her sea-green eyes full of determination. "Take me back to Drovers Bend. I want Ellsworth Pond in jail. I want to see him rot away the rest of his life behind bars or be hung. I've the proof for it now," she said.

Fargo heard Darcy's voice cut in and saw her swing from the tail of her wagon, her face still made of hurt and pride. "If she's going back, I am, too," Darcy said.

Athena spun on her. "Haven't you heard enough and seen enough? Why do you keep on? Face the facts," she flung at Darcy.

"I don't know all the facts. Neither do you," Darcy returned angrily. "You don't care about those missing pieces. I do."

Fargo cut in, his voice hard. "I care. I want the truth of it, once and for all. There's been too much killing for anything less," he said.

Athena's silence was a grudging admission. "My wagon's too shot up and splintered to make it back," Darcy said.

Fargo heard Herb Atkinson answer before he could reply. "I'm going back, too. I've no reason to go on now," the man said. "You can ride with me, Darcy. I'd be grateful for company."

"Good enough. I'll get my things together," Darcy said.

"Joe will ride with you," Fargo cut in, and drew a set of frowns. "We go back together and we'll never reach Ellsworth Pond," Fargo said. "He knows what it'll mean if Athena comes back. He'll have men riding the range, searching, waiting. You two and Joe will go on back ahead of us. They'll stop you and you tell them you're the only survivors. You tell them the Comanche wiped out the rest of the train and everybody with it."

"And then?" Darcy questioned.

"Go into Drovers Bend, take a room at the hotel, and

stay low. I'll give Pond a day or two to relax and feel safe," Fargo said.

"Those final answers?" Darcy pressed.

"I'll get them," he said. "Good or bad, I'll get them to you."

She nodded, acceptance in her eyes. He turned to Athena as Darcy went to fetch her belongings. "You ready to go?" he asked, and she nodded. "I'll get my horse," he said. He paused to wave at Henrietta and the others as they headed west, watched Joe swing in to ride point ahead of Herb Atkinson's wagon, and he moved alongside Athena as she started her team forward. "We'll circle around the long way," he said affably, and saw Athena's sidelong glance.

"I hope you're not getting any ideas," she slid out.

"About what?" he asked innocently.

"About our agreement. I said after it was all done with, and it's not done with yet," she said.

"No, you said when I got you the proof you wanted and you've got enough for that," Fargo corrected. "But I'm not one to quibble over unimportant things."

Her eyes narrowed at him. "You're being too nice, the way you were about letting poor Judith take the organ," she said. "You're up to something."

"There goes that suspicious nature of yours again," Fargo said, and looked hurt. He spurred the pinto on and rode ahead of her until he called a halt in the lowering afternoon sun. He'd made a long circle that returned them heading east again and he made camp under a cluster of white firs. Athena put down her bedroll, stretched out on it, arms behind her head, and Fargo saw her eyes studying him.

"You are a strange mixture of a man, Fargo," she commented. "Ornery, even rotten, difficult to deal with, and yet you put your life on the line for Henrietta."

"I told you, the best and the worst," Fargo said.

"When did Henrietta tell you about herself and her daughters?" she asked.

"The night before we reached Condor Pass," Fargo said.

A tiny frown stabbed Athena's forehead. "I woke up that night a little before dawn. I heard a noise and saw Henrietta outside her wagon. Is that when she came to you?"

"She was just coming back then. She came soon after camp settled down," Fargo said casually. "We spent a good piece of time together that night."

Athena's frown deepened. "What are you saying, Fargo?" she questioned.

"I'm saying that Henrietta's a damn remarkable woman," he answered. "In every way."

"Are you telling me that you and Henrietta Corn . . . ?" she stammered.

"Does that bother you?" he asked.

"My God," Athena gasped. "Darcy Dennison was bad enough, but Henrietta Corn, too?"

"Why not Henrietta?" Fargo said.

"Of course, why not Henrietta? Why not anybody?" Athena flung at him. "Age obviously doesn't make any difference to you."

"Not by itself. Henrietta's got twenty years on you, gray-blond hair and two daughters nearing womanhood, but you're not one-half the woman she is," Fargo said.

"You don't know anything of the kind," Athena shouted at him, sitting up straight, her face flushed.

"Hell I don't. There's the real thing and then there's imitation," he said.

"You bastard, Fargo," she screamed, swung a blow at him.

He blocked it easily and looked for a second as her seawater eyes blazed with green fire.

"Goddamn you," she hissed, flung herself forward, and brought her mouth hard on his. He felt her lips open, soft and moist, and her tongue darted forward, quick little lunges, almost desperate in intensity. Her fingers pulled buttons open and again he heard her angry murmuring. "Bastard," she said, "damn you." And she fell half over him as he rolled onto his back. She wriggled the shirt from her shoulders and pulled her mouth free of his for a moment, arched her graceful neck back. His eyes took in the very white, cream-soft breasts and he half-smiled, the smooth, unbroken roundness of them under her blouses suddenly explained. Faint pink circles bordered tiny tips that lay recessed, like little rose-colored pearls inside tiny circled cushions. He moved his hands across their flatness and she shuddered, fell on her back, and pulled him with her.

He bent his lips to one tiny recessed nipple, let his tongue circle the cream-soft cushion, and Athena's abdomen sucked inward with a shuddered gasp of pleasure. He caressed the little rose-tinted tip and felt it rise, a tiny movement, sudden soft-firmness in his mouth, just enough for him to suck into his lips.

"Oh, oh, ooooh," Athena murmured, and he felt her back arching, her hands pushing her skirt down. He shed clothes as he drew her beautifully smooth breast deep into his mouth, pulled back to admire her nakedness. He saw her cream-white body waiting, trembling, a lovely, round rib cage, hips nicely fleshed out, and a tiny mound of convex smoothness over the flat, small black triangle. Well-formed legs with succulent thighs stretched downward, a body unrealized and waiting, edging voluptuousness.

He ran his hands down the smoothness of her and she shuddered, drew her legs up together even as she trembled with pleasure, the response automatic. He pushed her legs down roughly and she whimpered in protest, then half-screamed as he drew his hand up between her thighs. "No, no . . . oh . . ." she murmured as her head tossed half-angrily from side to side. Her hands dug into his shoulders as he pressed his fingers upward, pushing the smooth softness of her legs open. He touched the dark place, a swift caress, and her scream came at once, full of wild joy. Again, her back arched and she pushed her pelvis upward. She flung herself against his hand and cried out angry words. "Bastard, damn bastard," he heard her gasped scream. She twisted her body, pushed the round breasts up at him. "Take them . . . take them," she murmured, and he put his mouth to their sweet softness and her arm pressed him hard against her. He felt her hand groping for the hardness of him and he guided her, brought the swollen lance against her, and her scream pierced the new night, joy and triumph, the ecstasy of discovery too long held back.

She pulled him to her and her words were choked out of her throat. "Please . . . please . . . oh, my God . . . please." He touched the soft, wet lips of darkness and she refused to wait, flinging herself against him, and he felt the tightness of her tear open and her scream was muffled against his chest, the pain of pleasure and the pleasure of pain. She pumped furiously against him, exploding all the waiting yesterdays in the fever of desire, and he thrust hard into her, her cries demanding, begging, entreating. He rolled onto his back, staying inside her, and she nodded feverishly as she straddled him. Her little belly sucked in and out as she pumped furiously atop him and he heard her tiny cries of protest as consuming ecstasy enveloped her and yet held back.

"Help me, damn you, oh, God, help me," she said into his chest as she continued to pump desperately. He pushed her over onto her back again and drew from her, a sudden, swift motion. She screamed in protest, smashed her hands against his chest. "No . . . no . . . damn you . . . no . . ." He saw her face twist in anguish and then he came to her again, moving slowly into her, and saw her body almost stiffen, her breath leave her in a long, shuddered sigh. She drew her hips back as he drew back, held his throbbing maleness at the very entrance of her warmth. He watched her eyes open, stare at him, deep green blue, watched the gathering come into their orbs. She flung herself forward as he rammed into her and he felt himself explode with her, pulled her breast into his mouth. Her legs pressed hard against his ribs as she heaved and twisted, entirely consumed, whispered sounds falling from her lips, ecstasy turned inward, and finally he felt her trembling cease, her body go limp.

But she held her legs hard against him, unwilling to release his still-swollen gift. He lay atop her, let quietness slip through her, and finally her legs dropped down and he drew from her, heard her sigh of disappointment. He let his eyes enjoy the new-woman beauty of her and she finally lifted herself up to let her arms encircle his chest. He saw the seawater eyes had turned a cool gray green again.

"Was that real enough?" she asked.

His smile was slow. "It was a good start," he said.

"Damn you, Fargo," she spit out, sat up, and he watched the smoothly rounded breasts lift. He reached out, pressed his mouth to one, found the tiny rose tip in its pillowed nest, and rubbed his tongue over it. The quiver coursed through her body instantly.

"Let's try it again. You need practice," he murmured. He felt her hand reach down along his muscled body in silent answer.

She finally slept beside him, satiated, wrapped in the happiness of new beginnings. He woke first with the new dawn, pulled on trousers, and watched her stir, rub sleep from her eyes. She stretched awake with a Cheshire-cat smug satisfaction in her eyes. She ran her hands over the smooth, lovely breasts, down along her torso, pressed them into her little belly, as if feeling her body for the first time. "Do we have to get started this early?" she murmured.

He shrugged, knelt down beside her. "Not really, come to think about it," he said, and she lay back, sighed happily as his mouth found her breasts.

It was midmorning when he rode the pinto beside the wagon. "How long before we get back to Drovers Bend?" she asked.

"A few days more. We'll make better time than when we left with the other wagons," he told her. "Sorry?" He laughed.

"Yes and no," she said honestly. "I want Pond. I want it finished."

"Soon enough," he said. "I'll try to keep your mind on other things till then."

"Please do," she said.

He kept his promise and the trip back was more than he'd hoped for, and the last afternoon was upon them when he guided the wagon into a shadowed covert in a sandstone pillar.

"We wait here till it gets dark. I want to reach Drovers Bend by night," he told her.

She nodded and he watched her slowly unbutton her shirt, her eyes blue green as they held on him. He came to her and felt the sudden urgency in her arms, which circled him, pulled him close. He was sorry when the night descended and he slowly pulled on clothes. He checked the big Colt, the grimness settling too quickly upon him. Athena drove the wagon in silence as they moved from the sandstone pillar. They were nearing Drovers Bend when she spoke.

"What about Darcy?" she asked.

"What about her?" he returned.

"What if she has to face the truth finally? What if those final answers hurt bad?" Athena pressed. "You going to comfort her?"

Fargo let a low laugh drift into the dark. "You're consistent, anyway," he said.

"What's that mean?" she pushed back.

"You started out jealous and you're ending up still jealous," he said.

"Bastard," she muttered.

Fargo saw the dark outline of Drovers Bend appear under the half-moon. "You know where Pónd lives?" he asked Athena.

"A small house on the other side of town," she said. "He's a loner, lives by himself, stays by himself."

Fargo veered off, took a circle around the side of the town, and moved in from the other end.

Athena peered into the night, pointed to a frame house standing by itself a quarter-mile from town. "That's it," she said.

"Leave the wagon here," he told her, reached over, and pulled her onto the pinto with him. He moved forward, the horse at a slow walk.

A single light burned in one of the windows of the house; Fargo halted the horse, lowered himself silently to the ground, and lifted Athena down. A short, wooden porch fronted the house and Fargo stole up to the lighted window, pressed himself close to the wall of the house, and edged a glance into the window. He saw Pond at a table, a ledger book in front of him, the lamp nearby. He peered harder, saw the man had a gun belt on. Fargo moved back, motioned to Athena, and she came to the porch. He whispered instructions to her and she nodded understanding, stepped onto the porch, and began to walk toward the window.

Fargo retreated to the other side of the house where another window gave him a glimpse of the room, just enough to see Pond at the table. Drawing the Colt, the Trailsman waited, heard Athena scrape her foot along the wall of the house. She was following orders, he grunted silently. She'd be positioned in front of the window now. Her foot scraped against the wall again and Fargo saw Pond look up, watched him stare forward, the frown sliding over his caricature of a face. He saw the man's mouth drop open, his tongue pass over his too-thick lips. Ellsworth Pond rose from the chair, still staring, and Fargo's smile was hard. The man saw Athena at the window, standing ghostlike in the moonlight, Athena Neils, killed by the Comanche.

Fargo's eyes narrowed as he saw Pond straighten, reach behind him, and his hands came back into view with the rifle. The man started around the corner of the table, his jaw still hanging open, moving for the window. Athena would have stepped back now, vanished, and Fargo took two long strides to the front of the house, crouched down in the shadows at the corner post. He saw the door flung open and Pond rush out, the rifle in his hand. The man peered up and down the porch, his jowls quivering.

"Drop the gun," Fargo called softly.

Pond stiffened, paused, then whirled, firing a blast in the direction of Fargo's voice. The shot came close enough—too close, as Fargo felt the wind of it pass his face. He saw Pond searching the darkness, bring the rifle up again, and the Colt spit out a single shot.

"Ow, Jesus," Pond screamed, and his left hand erupted in a shower of red. The rifle dropped to the ground and Fargo moved into sight in one long stride, the Colt aimed at Pond's midsection.

"Inside," Fargo growled, and the man backed through the doorway and into the room. Fargo followed, heard Athena hurrying up to come into the room beside him. Ellsworth Pond's overblown face stared at her, disbelief and confusion slowly turning into rage. "No ghost, Pond. You weren't seeing things," Fargo said. "You shouldn't believe everything you hear."

"Bitch," the man rasped. "Stinking, busybody bitch." He pressed his left hand against his shirt.

"Talk," Fargo said. "I want the whole of it."

"You don't get nothin'," the man flung back.

"Selling guns to the Indians is fifteen years. You might even get less with a good lawyer. But I'll put a bullet through your rotten head if you don't talk. You've three seconds to make your mind up," Fargo said. He pulled the hammer back on the Colt and the click was loud and clear in the stillness of the room. He saw Pond's face go chalk, his throat bob as he swallowed.

"What do you want to know?" Pond growled.

"You had Condor Pass all set up. What went wrong?" Fargo asked.

"The goddamn Indian was supposed to surprise the wagon train, catch them before they could fire off a shot," Pond said. "He was supposed to take their guns and make off with the wagons. That's how it worked the time before."

"A Comanche raid on a wagon train. They take the horses and the wagons and run. Nobody would ever suspect that it was a cover for a gun-smuggling operation. But something else happened this time. Why, dammit?"

"I don't know," Pond said, his eyes blinking.

Fargo's backhanded blow sent the man crashing into the wall with a cry of pain. The barrel of the Colt pressed into his forehead as he stood against the wall. "You've got one more chance," the big man hissed.

"All right, all right," Pond breathed, and Fargo took the Colt from his forehead. Pond wiped the trickle of blood from his mouth with the back of his right hand as he straightened up. "I got wind there might be trouble. It seems half the last rifles I sold him were no good," he said. "I didn't know that, but the bastard wouldn't believe it."

"That's why you pulled that last-minute sick act," Athena said. "That's why you sent your cousin in your place."

"I wasn't sure there'd be trouble. You hear a lot of things," Pond pleaded. "I wouldn't have let them all go if I knew for sure."

"You were afraid enough not to risk your neck going along," Fargo snapped. "You sniveling bastard. It still comes out murder." Pond shook his head in denial. "One more thing. Colonel Dennison. How much did he know?"

Contempt came into Pond's overblown face. "That fool," he spit out. "I sold him a bill of goods. I told him the government was trying to make peace with the Comanche without anyone knowing about it, and it was all a cover to give the Indians blankets and food. He bought it hook, line, and sinker. That's what comes from spending all your life in the army, believing what people tell you. I hired him as window dressing." Pond's face twisted angrily. "It would have all worked perfect, the way it did the time before, if the goddamn Indian had played his part right."

"You mean if you hadn't tried to cheat him with no-good rifles the last time," Fargo said. "Let's go, Pond. There's a jail cell waiting for you."

The man's eyes looked at Athena, flickered back to the big black-haired man. "I'm bleeding. Let me bandage my hand first."

"You can bleed to death for all I care," Fargo said. "Let's go."

Pond shrugged. "Can I take my jacket?" he asked, indicating the gray frock coat on the nearby hanger.

"Take it," Fargo said. He watched the man reach up with his right hand, lift the jacket from the hook, and slip his arm into it. Gingerly he slid his other arm into the sleeve. Fargo motioned to the door and Pond began to walk toward it as Athena went out first. Fargo saw Pond lift his right hand, half-turn to him. "Can I have a cigarette?" he asked.

"Suit yourself," Fargo muttered. Pond reached into

the pocket of his jacket, started to draw his hand out when he dived sideways across the porch. Fargo hurtled forward, smashed into Athena, and sent her sprawling off the porch as the two shots grazed her hair. He landed half atop her, spun onto his back to see Pond aiming the small, four-shot foreign pocket pistol again. The big Colt erupted, three explosions of sound, and Ellsworth Pond's caricature of a face became a caricature of a death mask as he sank to the ground, the gray frock coat suddenly turning red.

Fargo rose, pulled Athena up beside him. He turned away and strode to the pinto. There was no reason to stay. It was finished, once and for all. Athena remained silent until she rolled the wagon into Drovers Bend beside him as he pulled up before the hotel.

"I owe her an apology," she said. "He was a victim, as much as any of the others. Maybe more of a one."

"I'll give it to her for you," he said.

Athena's eyes were round. "She won't need comforting."

Fargo allowed a smile. "I guess not," he said.

She looked pleased. "I'll be at the house," she said. "Don't be too long."

"I won't. Don't have too many clothes on," he said as he swung from the pinto, watched her send the wagon hurrying away. He estimated he had at least two weeks of special pay to collect before moving on.

LOOKING FORWARD

The following is the opening section from the next novel in the exciting new *Trailsman* series from Signet:

THE TRAILSMAN #13: BLOOD CHASE

The Utah Territory, 1861, just southwest of Dead Horse Point.

There was something wrong, goddammit, Skye Fargo muttered silently as he peered over the ridge at the three men and the girl beside the campfire. His suspicions had become almost certainty and his lake-blue eyes narrowed as they scanned the darkness around the circle of light. The thick cockspur haws reached almost to the small clearing, their long thorns visible at the tops of their branches nearest the fire. His eyes moved to the girl and watched her red hair gleam copper in the firelight's glow. She stretched her long figure and the shadows underlined the fullness of her breasts beneath the white blouse.

Miss Ivy Thompson, twenty years old, tall, redheaded, china-blue eyes, and something was still very wrong, he muttered to himself again. He relaxed his big, hard-muscled frame. There was no hurry now that he'd caught up with the quartet. They'd settled in for the night and Fargo let his thoughts go back to the beginning, his meeting with Morley Thompson at the man's big ranch house.

"My daughter will arrive at the Dobbsville hotel on

the stage from Wyoming," Morley Thompson had told him as he described the girl. "She's been back East at a fancy finishing school. Her mother insisted on that. She loves horses and fancy riding and she's headstrong." Morley Thompson had paused, his eyes growing narrow. "But I've received information that some people don't want her visiting me and may try to stop her."

"Some people?" Fargo had interrupted.

Morley Thompson allowed a cool smile. A large man with gray-streaked hair, he had a face a little too heavy for handsomeness but with plenty of room for authority. "Who and why are not important at this time," the man said. "What is important is that I've been told that you are the man who can get her to me safe and sound. In fact, you were highly recommended."

"I can try," Fargo remarked.

"My information tells me to have full confidence in the Trailsman," the man said, and Fargo made no comment. "I've a small note here to my daughter, telling her I've sent you for her," Morley Thompson said, and pushed the square little envelope out.

Fargo took it, and the rest of the arrangements had been quickly concluded, five hundred dollars and his hand to bring Ivy Thompson to her father safe and sound.

It was a three-day ride to Dobbsville and he'd arrived at the hotel a day early, only to have the desk clerk tell him that Ivy Thompson had been kidnapped out of her room the night before.

"Three mean-looking gunslingers," the small, bespectacled man had told him. "They came in here last night and took her out screaming and kicking. She made one hell of a lot of noise yelling how she was being kidnapped before they got her onto a horse and lit out with her. They were gone before the sheriff got here, but plenty of folks heard her, so you can ask any of them."

Fargo felt the frown digging into his forehead as he listened to the man. "Which way?" he asked after a moment.

"They went northwest out of town, along the Clay Ridge Road," the desk clerk said.

Fargo had left at once, sending the gleaming black-and-white Ovaro along the only road leading northwest from the town. Aptly named, the red clay held hoofprints clearly, but too many of them. It was over an hour before he could pick up their tracks from all the others imprinted onto the porous soil. The four horses staying close together made their own pattern of tracks, and he carefully picked his way along after the hoofmarks. The task grew easier when they left the red-clay road and moved upward into the sloping hillsides. Night came to stop him from following the trail farther, but he remembered how he'd already found himself frowning at the tracks.

When morning came, he picked up the tracks again, the four sets of hoofprints riding together, and he followed with his brow furrowing again; the trail, to him, was not merely a set of tracks but a picture, a message, for he saw where others only looked, observed where others only followed. He was the Trailsman.

They rode into the Smokey Tree foothills and he halted where they'd stopped at a pond, swung down from the pinto to the ground. He ran his fingers over the footprints at the edge of the pond, and when he rose, he stared down at the marks for a moment longer before returning to the saddle, his lips pursed. In the late afternoon, where the hills grew deeper, he reined the pinto to a halt again and leaned forward in the saddle, his eyes sweeping the ground. A slope of grass lay trampled in a wide swath. Elk, he grunted, a big herd. They'd come down the slope fast, crushing the grass hard into the ground, and one of the riders had been cut off. He saw the horse's hoofprints as it had backed off, halted to wait. Slowly Fargo had crossed the flattened grass, his brow pulled down in thought as he'd followed the tracks until darkness once again called a halt to trailing.

Fargo snapped thoughts off, pulled himself straighter, and gazed down at the campfire, now burned into glowing embers. He had caught up with them at dusk, just as they'd settled into the little hollow, and the words echoed inside him again. Something was wrong. He rose, left the pinto, and began to move forward in his long, loping gait, silent as a wolf on the prowl. He moved into the stand of cockspur haws, slowed to make his way carefully through the sharp, thorn-studded branches. He dropped to the ground as he reached the edge of the hollow, his eyes moving over each of the still forms.

Skye Fargo became motionless and let his ears tune in on the nearest man, listened to the man's heavy, rhythmic breathing, and then tuned in to the next figure. He heard the half-snoring sounds of air being taken in through an open mouth in heavy sleep. Fargo half-turned and picked up the sounds of the girl even, slightly shallow breathing as she lay on her side in sleep. He tuned in on the third man under the saddle blanket, listened, and a thin, cold smile edged his lips. No sound of sleep reached his ears, only the soft, even sound of very awake breathing. They were being clever. No one posted on watch but a sleeping decoy.

Fargo crawled along the edge of the trees, using his elbows to pull himself forward with noiseless little motions. He passed the decoy under the saddle blanket, continued to circle the little hollow. It was painfully slow and he had to force away the desire to hurry his progress, but he finally reached the edge of the hollow behind the figure. He rose to his feet, drew the big Colt .45 from its holster, and paused to scan the hollow again. The four horses were strung together a half-dozen yards away, and as he watched, he saw two of the mounts moving restlessly, sensing his presence. He grimaced as he began to move out of the trees, a crouching, silent stride, toward the back of the man under the saddle blanket. He had nearly reached the figure when one of the horses whinnied, a sudden, nervous whinny immediately picked up by another. Fargo saw the man sit up, start to spin around toward the horses.

"Damn," Fargo hissed under his breath, saw the gun in the man's hands. He took a single stride as the man saw his dark shape, brought the barrel of the heavy Colt down with a swift, savage blow. The man's forehead cracked open in a jagged line of red and he fell backward. But his finger had been on the trigger of his gun and it tightened. The gun exploded into the air and Fargo dived to the ground as the other two men came awake, rolling, spinning, guns in their hands. He glimpsed the girl sitting up as he rolled away from three shots that winged through the dark at him.

One of the two figures rose to one knee, barely silhouetted against the fire's embers, but it was enough for the Trailsman. He fired, and the figure arched backward and landed on the glowing embers. A small cloud of sparks and ashes flew into the air, to cast a moment's glow of light around the body that had made its own poor-man's funeral pyre. Fargo rolled on the ground as the third man fired, and he heard the two shots hit the ground where he'd been. He came to a halt on his stomach, the Colt outstretched as he sought to find a bead on the third man and saw the man yanking the girl backward against him as a shield.

"Let go," he heard her cry out.

"Shut up," the man said, lifted his voice to call out. "Shoot and she gets it," he said.

"No, you son of a bitch," Fargo heard the girl yell,

but the man got to his feet, pulling her up in front of him, one arm around her waist. He moved backward toward the horses, and Fargo slipped into the darker shadows, retreating until he reached the tree line. He ran then, crouched over, along the edge of the trees, and he could hear the kidnapper had reached the horses. He kept running until he was at the far turn of the clearing. The sound of hooves breaking into an instant gallop thudded through the dark and Fargo crouched, waiting, saw the horse come into sight racing toward where he crouched. The rider was alone, lying flat across the horse's back. He'd discarded the girl as only useless baggage now. It had been too hasty a decision, Fargo snorted silently, contemptuously. With the girl on the horse, a shot would have been far too risky.

He raised the big Colt, aimed, followed the path of the dark shape clinging to the horse's back. He fired, a single shot, and the figure leaped convulsively, fingers curling tight around the reins. The man's hands stayed closed around the reins as his body slipped from the horse, fingers locked in a death vise. His body was still lifelessly bouncing along the ground beside the galloping horse as the animal vanished into the darkness.

Fargo rose to his feet, turned to the little clearing. "Ivy Thompson," he called, and there was only silence. "It's all right. You can come out," he said, holstering the gun. He waited, saw the movement near the side where the other horses were still tethered. He broke into a run, reached the horses just as she pulled herself onto one of the mounts and frantically tried to unravel the tethers. He closed a big hand over her wrist, soothed the horse with his other hand. "I said it's all right," Fargo told the girl. "Simmer down."

He reached up, put an arm around her waist, and lifted her to the ground. She felt nicely soft under his hand, the bottom curve of full breasts resting against his fingers.

"Who are you?" she murmured, staring at him as he set her down.

"Fargo, Skye Fargo," he said. "Your pa sent me to fetch you in Dobbsville. Seems your late friends beat me to it."

He turned from her, walked to where the saddles lay on the ground, and threw one onto a brown gelding, tightened the cinch. "Why'd you try to run?" he asked almost casually.

"I didn't know who you were," she answered.

"Makes sense," he commented. "No point in being kidnapped twice, is there?"

"No," she said as he started to lead the horse away. He walked to where he'd left the strikingly marked Ovaro, waited for a moment as the girl came up. She met his glance in silence and he motioned to the gelding.

"Where are we going?" she asked as she swung onto the horse.

"Away from here, first," he said. "Things are sort of dead around here."

He started up the hilly slope, rode until he found a small hollow almost surrounded by a stand of alders. He slid to the ground and gathered enough loose dry tinder to get a fire going quickly.

Ivy Thompson dismounted as the fire caught, flared up to light the little hollow. She still eyed him warily, Fargo saw.

"Relax." He smiled. "Your pa really did send me for you." Fishing in his jacket, he handed the note to her, studied her as she read it.

Beside the brightly burning fire, he had a chance to see her well for the first time, and his eyes took in the red hair, much brighter than it had seemed from a distance, her face with a touch of coarseness in it, a hardness in her blue eyes. Her breasts hung a little heavily on the inexpensive cotton blouse and she looked up from the note with a little shrug.

"I guess you're the real thing," she said.

"I am." He smiled. "Now I'm going to get some sleep. We've a long piece of riding tomorrow before I get you to your pa."

He unsaddled the horses, laid out his bedroll, and handed her a blanket. She nodded as she lay down with it, and he stretched out, took off boots and shirt. "Those three gunslingers who took you, they say who sent them?" he asked almost idly.

"No," she murmured. "They didn't talk much at all."

"You have any ideas about it, Ivy?" he questioned.

"No," she answered.

He settled himself down, turned on his side, facing her. "Well, maybe your pa will have some thoughts on it," he said. "Get some sleep."

He let himself fall asleep with that mountain cat's half-sleep he'd mastered long ago, the mind wrapped in slumber while the senses remained alert, subconsciously aware of every sound. It was near dawn when he snapped awake, saw the girl moving toward the horses. "Something wrong, Ivy?" he asked, and she turned at once.

"I wanted some water. My throat's dry and scratchy," she said. "I've a canteen."

"Sure thing," he said, lay back, and watched her as she drank a few mouthfuls, then walked back to the blanket. He watched her move with a swaying, sensuous motion and she sank down to pull the blanket around herself again. He closed his eyes and returned to sleep until the morning sun filtered its way into the little hollow.

He woke her as he pulled on boots and she sat up,

rubbed sleep from her eyes. He found a small stream nearby and let her wash and freshen herself. They were riding northeast before the sun edged the top of the hills and he set a steady, ground-eating pace. She tended to jounce as shè rode, he noticed, and she continued to remain quiet, almost sullen. It didn't bother him any. He wanted to make time, not talk.

He halted once at a cluster of wild, ripe papaws, which made a satisfying meal, their creamy sweetness serving as both food and drink. It was nearly dusk when he came into sight of Morley Thompson's large ranch house, perched atop a hill. He gave Ivy an encouraging smile and saw her eyes peering hard at the house. Reining up in front of the doorway, he swung from the pinto with a loose, easy motion. "Wait here. Let me see if your pa's home," he said.

The girl nodded and he walked to the tall, pinewood door, had just raised his hand to knock when it opened and Morley Thompson faced him. The man's thick brows were pulled down as he stared past Fargo to the girl on the horse outside.

"Had some delays getting back," Fargo said.

"What the hell is this, Fargo?" Morley Thompson growled. "That's not my daughter."

Fargo glanced back at the girl. "I know that. I thought you might know who the hell she is," he said calmly.